"What Am I to Do with You?"

Lord Rothe's voice had lost some of its sharpness, and the warmth that scraped low in his tone left her nerveless for a moment. She stared up at his face, seeing only his shadowed eyes and the sharp, pale angles of the hollows of his cheeks.

"Do with me?" she answered, feeling oddly breathless. Then all the old warnings blared. She was a sensible woman far past the age of infatuations and foolishness and longings. She was not a girl to be led astray by her own weakness.

Straightening, she tried to disengage her hands from his, but it was like trying to climb out of the softest feather bed. The more she tugged, the more she seemed to be engulfed in his grip and the less inclined she felt to leave.

Turning away finally allowed her to pull her hands free of his; then she knew that she had better say something or he might think he had upset her.

She put on a bright tone. "I suppose it would look badly to have the governess frozen solid in this ruined wing. I would probably end up haunting Rothe House, and ghosts are such a dreadful nuisance."

He took her hand, his grip light but insistent, and his hold upon her drew her down to sit next to him. She curled her feet tight under her, as if making herself smaller would diminish the awareness of him that almost hummed along her skin.

"Ghosts are more than a nuisance, Miss Midden. And so is a governess who will not have a care for herself. Did you not find your room to your liking? Is that why you wander the house? I can find you another if you prefer. One with lovely, thick, warm carpets."

She could not stop the smile that relaxed her face. She wondered, how was she supposed to stay on her guard against a man who seemed oblivious to the potency of his charm? "My room is lovely. It is nothing to do with that. It is just that I often do not sleep well."

A smile lifted his voice. "I can hardly believe that it is due to a guilty conscience over a scandalous past."

She bit her lower lip and watched him, her eyes straining to see his expression, terrified that somehow he had guessed. But he said nothing more. Slowly she let out the breath she had been holding. He did not know. He could not. . . .

BOOK YOUR PLACE ON OUR WEBSITE AND MAKE THE READING CONNECTION!

We've created a customized website just for our very special readers, where you can get the inside scoop on everything that's going on with Zebra, Pinnacle and Kensington books.

When you come online, you'll have the exciting opportunity to:

- View covers of upcoming books
- Read sample chapters
- Learn about our future publishing schedule (listed by publication month *and author*)
- Find out when your favorite authors will be visiting a city near you
- Search for and order backlist books from our online catalog
- Check out author bios and background information
- Send e-mail to your favorite authors
- Meet the Kensington staff online
- Join us in weekly chats with authors, readers and other guests
- Get writing guidelines
- AND MUCH MORE!

Visit our website at
http://www.zebrabooks.com

A COMPROMISING SITUATION

Shannon Donnelly

ZEBRA BOOKS
Kensington Publishing Corp.
http://www.zebrabooks.com

ZEBRA BOOKS are published by

Kensington Publishing Corp.
850 Third Avenue
New York, NY 10022

All Kensington titles, imprints and distributed lines are available at special quantity discounts for bulk purchases for sales promotion, premiums, fund raising, educational or institutional use.

Special book excerpts or customized printings can also be created to fit specific needs. For details, write or phone the office of the Kensington Sales Manager: Kensington Publishing Corp., 850 Third Avenue, New York, NY 10022, Attn. Special Sales Department. Phone: 1-800-221-2647.

First Printing: November, 2000
10 9 8 7 6 5 4 3 2 1

Printed in the United States of America

For Nedra,
who always believed
and who read everything

One

The three girls laughed as they fell down in the spring grass, indifferent to what this might be doing to their white pinafores, and Miss Maeve Midden, suddenly and unaccountably, wished that these were her girls. Her mouth curved with a rare smile. The unaccountability for the feeling was easy enough to trace. She had long ago put away wishes for children or a family of her own. She had put it away as she had put away every other hope a young girl cherishes. In this world, a governess had no use for dreams.

However, with a breath of warmth in the March breeze and the sun brilliant on the green lawns and a lively al fresco party before her view, the sharp longing in her chest would not stay boxed in its tight compartment. It wormed its way out and crept up to her throat, winding up to her travel-weary mind like some clever, intimate serpent. And, as did the serpent in Eve's garden, it whispered insidious thoughts to her.

Why couldn't these be her girls, even if only to teach? Why, by the time the youngest was out of the schoolroom, the eldest would have married and would more than likely have a child who would be of an age to need a governess. She might stay with such a family for years . . . she might have a home again.

A small sigh escaped, and she only knew that it had slipped past her guard when she heard it echo in the elegant drawing room in which she stood. She shook her head and started to turn away from the open casement windows that reached to the floor. But the smell of cut grass and warming earth slipped in through the parted French windows, and she gave in to the guilty indulgence of picturing a very large family of girls, all in great need of a governess. That was what she needed. Oh, how very badly she needed them.

Three positions in less than three years was beginning to make her seem . . . what was the word Mr. Jessup had used when she had first presented herself at his agency? Ah, yes . . . *unsteady,* as if she were a chair with a short leg on one side, or a carriage with a wobbly wheel. It seemed not to matter that the brevity of her employment was not due to any lapse in the performance of her duties. It did not matter at all. No, a woman only had to be born to accept blame and consequences, she thought bitterly.

She chided herself for that thought. She had vowed not to regret her choices. Nine years ago, she had made a promise to herself to only look ahead. And that was exactly where she should be looking, with both eyes firmly open and fixed on the reality of her present life.

She turned from the window and pulled back her shoulders, feeling as she did the tug of strained seams in her second-best gown. She smoothed the brown wool and took a less shallow breath. Over eight years in service had worn out the dress, and her as well if she was now giving in so easily to such grim musings.

She touched the letter in her reticule for a bit of luck, listening to the paper crumple. The letter had been few in its particulars. The hurried scrawl read almost as if Mr. Jessup—of Hastings, Hastings and Jessup Employment Agency, Pultney Bridge, Bath—had dashed off the missive while the postman was calling out his cry for the last post. It had at least been particular in noting that the situation called for a governess to a "young lady." Emphasis on the singular, Maeve thought. She thought back to the girls on the lawn. They must be friends who were visiting, or perhaps a neighbor's children.

She glanced around the room, taking in its rich appointments, the gold silk wall coverings and fashionable furnishings which showed off Mr. Chippendale's fine workmanship. One girl—and perhaps a greatly indulged child, to judge by this display of wealth.

Maeve imagined the house must have been in the family for centuries, for the stone exterior seemed a jumble of styles that somehow managed to find a harmony between its fortified walls and more modern wings, its towers and chimneys and its vast number of mullioned windows. This room itself was large, with a plastered ceiling and a pleasant view of the north lawns.

It struck Maeve as a house well suited to a large and boisterous family, but if she could not hope for a large family, then perhaps, at least, the daughter of the house was "young." Very young and greatly in need of a governess.

A girl's voice cut into Maeve's speculations, shrilling into the room through the open windows. "But I tell you, I am too old for a governess! I won't have it. I just won't!"

Oh, dear. It sounded as if the "young lady" was not that young after all, but was definitely quite that spoilt.

A slow, deep baritone followed the girl's pettish soprano. "When your opinion is required, I shall inform you. Until then, you shall do as you are told. And you are to have a governess until you learn some manners."

A chill which had nothing to do with changeable spring weather chased along Miss Midden's skin under her wool dress. She knew a tyrant when she heard one, and this man had the inflexibility of hundred-year oak in his voice.

Just as she thought that, he spoke again, his voice gentling with patience, even if it did sound fraying on the edges. "Now, is this to become another of your unanswerable arguments, with you saying you won't while I say you will? Or will you act your age and do as you are bid?"

"I am sixteen, and I won't be treated as a child!"

Sixteen, Miss Midden thought, her hopes sinking to the worn soles of her traveling boots. Why must they always be sixteen and a year away from their debut to society? Well, this position just would not do, not for her or the girl.

"You will be treated as you act, Clarissa . . . ," the man said, his voice so sharp now that Maeve cringed for Clarissa. She knew too well what it was to be on the receiving side of such unkindness.

The gentleman's next words had Maeve's sympathy changing into alarm as he shouted, "Put down that flower pot, miss! You will not demonstrate the very reason why you need a—"

Pottery crashed against stone, and then the French windows slammed fully open.

Between the billowing curtains, a girl stood, trembling with anger, her expression both cross and startled. Golden hair, in a riot of curls, framed a stormy, heart-shaped face. Blue eyes the color of a summer sky swam with tears, and more tears trembled on long, dark lashes. She was a little thing, but so perfect that Maeve stared in open-mouthed awe of such beauty.

Then Maeve glimpsed the architect of the girl's distress.

He stood directly behind the girl, seeming as startled as Maeve by her sudden inclusion in this argument.

He was dark. Very dark. The only lightness in him came from his white shirt and cravat. A black coat lay smooth over wide shoulders. Black riding breeches and boots covered his legs. His hair and eyes were also black, or so dark a brown as to seem inky, and years under a hot sun had tanned his skin to nut brown. He had a lean face and a strong nose, and a forceful aura of command came into the room with him.

His dark eyes narrowed with irritation as they rested on Maeve, and his black eyebrows pulled tight together.

"I beg your pardon," Maeve said, hastily dropping a curtsy and lowering her gaze to the floral pattern on the carpet. A governess did not eavesdrop—or if she did, she had better be wise enough not to admit it—and a governess never, but never, boldly stared at her betters. "I am Miss Midden. The footman . . . that is . . . well, I was told to wait here."

She looked up, floundering suddenly as she met the stormy blue eyes of the girl—Clarissa, the gentleman had called her. The softly ringing tones of that name suited her angelic beauty. Maeve felt a tug of empathy for the troubled child, for she could still remember her own desire to grow up far faster than had been wise.

"I have come at a bad time, I see. And I probably should not have come at all," Maeve said, blurting out the honest truth. She turned and met the gentleman's dark-eyed stare. Her nerve faltered. The set of his determined jaw made him look an uncomfortable man to go against. But what choice did she have? She simply could not take on yet another short-term employment.

She stepped forward, her wool skirts softly hushing. "I am sorry for intruding. Mr. Jessup seems to have made a mistake in sending me here, for I—"

"Miss Midden."

The man's voice cracked across the room, startling Maeve again, throwing off her entire train of thought. The golden-haired Clarissa swung around to shoot a look of burning resentment at him.

"I am Colonel Derhurst. This is my niece, Clarissa Derhurst. Make your curtsy, miss."

Clarissa sullenly bobbed and then, chin lowered, continued to glare at her uncle.

"Derhurst?" Maeve asked, both confused and a touch relieved. "Oh, but that must be the mistake. I was engaged by Mr. Jessup of Hastings, Hastings and Jessup Employment Agency for Lord Rothe's household."

"Yes, I am Lord Rothe," the dark gentleman said, his expression turning even darker. "Formerly colonel in His Majesty's Rifles."

"I don't need a governess," Clarissa said again, flinging out this graceless phrase as if it were a gauntlet slapped down for a challenge.

However, Maeve saw the troubled look that haunted the back of Clarissa's defiant stare. She went at once to the girl's side, unable to ignore that unspoken plea for aid and comfort.

"Of course you do not," she said, choosing agreement as the surest way to cast a damper on any argument. "And I came expecting a child, not such a grown young lady as yourself. So since this is not a situation that suits either of us, I will leave, and I am sorry if my arrival caused you any distress."

The storm clouds hesitantly parted in Clarissa's eyes, but her uncle interrupted.

"Nonsense. Whatever you expected, Miss Midden, I am certain we can reach an agreement as to your employment here. Clarissa, you may wait in your rooms while we discuss this. Miss Midden, please come with me to my study."

He strode briskly to the main door and held it open, a look on his face that boded ill for any who crossed his orders.

Clarissa stood for a moment, her eyes glittering, her just budding bosom rising and falling with agitation. "Oh, how I wish you were dead instead of my father!"

With that she ran from the room.

Staring after the girl, the colonel muttered, "That makes two of us."

Maeve glanced at him, wondering if he was regretting the loss of his brother, or the burden of his niece.

He straightened as soon as her gaze fell on him, and gestured to the doorway. "Please, this way, Miss Midden."

She had never known anyone who could make such a simple request sound like such a complete order. However, after so many years in service, she knew how to obey.

Lowering her eyes again, she stepped into the hall and followed the colonel to a smaller room that looked onto a hedge-garden. She tried to keep her eyes respectfully downcast as she stepped into the room, but the odors of tobacco and books and leather teased her nose. She glanced up, taking in the sight of oak bookcases that rose up to a ceiling where plaster shaped an intricate design of garlands and rosettes. Leather armchairs faced each other beside a cheerful fire that took the chill off the room, and another large leather chair sat behind an enormous mahogany desk.

His lordship strode to the desk, with its tidy stacks of papers, his boots muffled by a deep Oriental carpet.

Maeve stood and waited. Her heart pounded uncomfortably in her chest. Her bonnet had started to give her a headache. Oh, what had Mr. Jessup landed her in this time? And how was she to convince Lord Rothe, Colonel Derhurst, or whatever he wished to be called, that this was all a mistake?

"Sit," he said, gesturing to one of the leather armchairs.

Goaded by his curt tone, she asked, "Am I to take that as an 'at ease,' sir?"

The corner of his mouth jerked up and then fell again. Now that she was near enough to see his features, she noticed that he had a sensitive mouth, well shaped with a full lower lip. It was a pity that he continually pulled its shape into a grim line. Sun might have darkened his complexion, ruining it, but he had a lean, intelligent face, with a high forehead and strong cheekbones. He was too thin, she decided. His cheeks seemed almost gaunt. And the energy in him could unnerve anyone, for it filled and overflowed the room.

He was, overall, an uncomfortable, unyielding man, and the sooner she ended her association with him and this household, the sooner she could find a lasting position.

"At ease, indeed," he remarked. Then he strode to the windows, where he stood with his hands clasped behind his back. "You have a male relative in the army, I take it?"

"No. My familiarity with the term comes from my last but one house. The youngest son was quite army mad."

He turned to look at her, his dark eyes narrowing again, either with disapproval or perhaps to sum her up, she could not quite decide. Then he strode back to his desk.

"Sit or stand as suits you. You will forgive me if I sit while I go over your papers. Mr. Jessup assured me your references are in order. I've drawn up a schedule for you to follow and I wish to make clear—"

"Sir!" she said, growing exasperated with him.

He looked up, then frowned again. "There is a problem with my giving you employment, Miss Midden?"

"Yes, there most certainly is. The problem is that . . . well, I am looking for a position with younger children."

He stared at her blankly. She felt her mouth dry under that unwavering stare, and her skin itched. She resisted the urge to fidget.

"Have you perhaps considered hiring a companion for your niece?" she asked. "A girl nearer to Clarissa in age?"

"I have considered any number of things, including shipping her off to one of those damn . . . those dashed finishing schools for ladies, only her mother would hold a weeping marathon at the thought of being parted from her 'dear angel.' "

"But if her mother is alive, why can she not—"

"Lady Rothe, my sister-in-law, does not leave her rooms."

Miss Midden blinked at such an absurd idea. "Not ever?" she asked, her curiosity stirred.

"Never . . . or at least the servants report she hasn't left them since my brother died last year. They have the devil of a time cleaning around her and that pack of yapping lapdogs she keeps."

"Poor Clarissa," she said softly, thinking of that high-strung girl, alone in this house with an unsympathetic uncle, a mother lost in grief, and perhaps no company her own age. No wonder she was troubled and acting up a bit.

A sharp, derisive laugh drew her attention back to the colonel. "Poor Clarissa? We will see if you are still saying so a month from now."

"Sir . . . Colonel . . . my lord . . . I do not plan to stay a month."

He folded his hands on his desk and stared at her with those dark, sardonic eyes. This time she did fidget. She twisted the strings of her reticule around one gloved finger.

"And how do you plan to leave?" he asked. "My carriage brought you here from York. My carriage is the only way back. And in this part of West Yorkshire, you are not likely to find transportation for hire."

She lifted her chin. "If you were to be so unkind as to deny me transport, I do have legs and can walk. A few miles—"

"It's nearly thirty miles."

"Thirty or three hundred, I am not averse to hard work!"

"Good. Then you should stand up well to the demands my niece and her mother put upon you." He turned back to his papers. "The schedule is here, along with your payment in advance for the first year. If you decide you have had your fill of my niece in a month's time—and I would not blame you if you do cry craven—then you may leave us with my blessing." He glanced up. The corner of his mouth lifted a fraction and his dark eyes gleamed. "You may also leave in my carriage."

That gleam in his eyes and the slight twisting of his mouth must be what passed for humor in him, she decided. It looked remarkably like sarcasm. No wonder he so irritated his niece. He could irritate a saint.

She glanced down at the packet on his desk, twisting her hands together. A year's salary . . . in advance. And she only had to stay the month. Oh, the man was a devil to tempt her with so much money. Why, with such funds, she might even actually be able to afford a few weeks on her own with nothing to do and no one to answer to. And a new dress. Her mouth almost watered.

Straightening, she met his stare. "It would be wrong for me to take your money without earning it. And I am looking for a position with young children."

"Clarissa only looks grown. I assure you she could match any babe's tantrums, so you may as well take the money and stay," he said, frowning as if she was making a complicated matter of something painfully simple.

He got up and came around the desk. Her impression that he was too thin vanished, for in close proximity he seemed to tower over her. He was very broad of shoulder, and solid muscle lay encased under his dark clothing. She would not be intimidated, however.

"My lord, I—"

"Please, call me Colonel or call me Derhurst. I feel damn, I mean dashed silly being called my lord, and I am forever wanting to look behind me to see who is really being addressed. I am even still signing my letters Derhurst."

He seemed so exasperated by his own title that she had to look down to suppress a smile. "Colonel, this is quite an impossible situation."

"Only because you are making it so," he said, and then he gave a deep sigh.

She glanced up. He had stepped back to the window and stood there with one hand dragging his hair back. It was an absentminded gesture, a habitual one, she would guess. It gave an unexpected flash of insight into his thoughts. Clarissa was not the only beleaguered soul in this house.

That intangible air of command which charged the space around him did not abate, but doubt shadowed his eyes. He still looked the perfect military man—it was etched into his erect bearing, his curt language. But the feeling swept through her that he was also a man struggling to come to terms with a world turned inside out. His brother had died, obviously leaving him a family he seemed not to know how to manage and an inheritance he must not have expected. She knew from her own past the panic of being flung into a strange world, and sympathy for him rocked her heart.

But she could not afford to think of others before herself. These people had property and family. In time, they would all learn to cope with their new situation and loss. She had. While she . . . well, if she stayed with them, it would be for a year at most. She would not go with them to London. She *could* not. Then it would be four positions in four years, and where would she go next? No, she could ill afford the luxury of sympathy for others, she told herself sharply. She lived in a hard-hearted world. She also must be hard-hearted.

The colonel straightened, glancing around him as if realizing that he stood in a house, not a field tent. He frowned, then went to his desk. He did not look at her, and Maeve had the impression that he needed those few moments to reassemble that facade of iron control.

"Miss Midden," he began after a moment, his tone even. "Your conscience is commendable, but I urge you to take my offer. I have money, but I have neither the time nor the desire to deal with the vapors produced by a sixteen-year-old hoyden. While you, to put it bluntly, have time and need money."

"Colonel, you almost sound as if you wish your niece were a private under your command whom you could deal with by court-martial or flogging." The reproof slipped out before she realized, and then she pressed her lips tight together. She did not care if she lost this position by offending him, but she could not afford the habit of speaking her own mind.

He glanced up at her, his eyes narrowed again, but she felt proof against that stare of his now that she had seen the uncertainty it hid.

"Do not underestimate the value of a flogging to re-form someone's character," he said. Then he asked, his voice sharp, "How long have you been a governess, Miss Midden?"

"Nearly nine years," she answered with a touch of pride that she had lasted that long. "Almost six with an academy in Bath and three with private families."

"Well, in that time I would have thought you would have learned not to be impertinent."

That did it. Habit or no, the man needed to be shown that others had feelings—herself included—and he could not simply ride roughshod over everyone.

"The truth is sometimes impertinent," she said, a long-dormant anger awakening in her. "But that does not make it any less the truth. And I am not at all surprised that you find your niece difficult to manage, for you order and demand when you need to listen and understand."

The amused gleam came back to his eyes. "That is exactly why I need you, Miss Midden. All I know is how to order and demand. I am, as you accuse me, an unbending man who can command a brigade, but I am lost when it comes to dealing with one single girl. Please, stay at least until I might find someone to take your place. Will you not grant me that small compromise?"

Logic urged her to listen to him, even as her heart warned her that staying held too many dangers. She became attached far too easily to places and to people. But how attached could she become in a month? And how lovely to have the luxury of looking for a new position with a present salary assured.

She took a breath, feeling her dress pinch around the bust. She stared at the packet of money on his desk.

"I will make this bargain with you, sir. I will stay as a paid companion to Clarissa just so long as it takes me to find a new position. I cannot in good conscience take a year's salary, but you may reimburse me for my work and for the expense of my coming here, and you may frank my letters of application."

"Can I do that?" he asked, frowning suddenly, a deep furrow appearing between his dark eyebrows.

"Do what? Frank a letter? Well, if you are indeed a lord, you should be able to sign your name to any letter for its free post."

"Damn . . . I beg pardon." He pinched the bridge of his nose. "Here I've been laying my letters out, waiting for one of the servants to post them, only they're waiting for me to sign them. No wonder the pile grows daily."

Maeve bit her lip and fought to keep from making any comment. Oh, the poor man. He really was quite lost at being a lord. However, he wanted a governess for his niece, not for himself, so it was not for her to offer advice.

"Well, at least it's settled between us. You are staying."

He rose and came to stand before her, so that she had

to look up at him, and for the first time, he smiled, really smiled. It transformed his face, softening the harsh lines, allowing her to see how attractive his mouth could be when it curved. His eyes lit so that they glowed like black opals.

"Thank you, Miss Midden," he said, his voice so low that it vibrated in her chest.

Maeve's mind stopped working. She could only dumbly stare back at him, her face flushed hot and a curious tightness in her chest.

Then he turned away. "I'll ring for someone to show you to the Blue Room, where you will stay."

She dropped a hasty curtsy before she turned and fumbled her way out of the room.

Outside of his study, she slumped against the oak door, holding tight to the brass doorknob, needing its support as she waited for the footman to arrive and show her to her room.

Oh, you silly, silly girl. After all these years, you would think that you of all people would be immune to the havoc that can be caused by masculine charm. But it seemed she was not immune. And who would credit that the very stiff, tyrannical Colonel Derhurst, the lord who did not feel himself a lord, could offer up such a warm and charming smile.

However, she had fallen once for a man's careless smiles, and once was enough to risk and lose a heart. She was not going to do so again.

Andrew sat at his desk, watching his steward's three daughters romp upon the east lawn. He knew he ought to be studying his ledgers, or looking at the architect's plans to rebuild the wing that had burnt in his grandfather's time—yet another task Phillip had undertaken but never quite finished.

Poor Phillip . . . and damn Phillip. Why did he, of all men, have to go and die? He'd been a hale forty-six two summers ago when Andrew had last been home upon leave. Phillip had barely sprouted his first gray hairs in his thinning dark hair, and he had talked endlessly about how he and Dorothy still hoped for a boy, and perhaps this year would be the one in which they produced a sibling for Clarissa. As with so many of Phillip's plans, that one had also been more talk than action.

It was a damn strange world, Andrew mused, that took one man from his home and left another one behind who should have died on some battlefield years ago. The world also seemed to have served Miss Midden her own ration of odd turns, if he knew anything of the matter.

Her current position as a governess might force her to spike her guns, but he'd seen her biting off her first thoughts, and that flush of irritation she had fought down. She might bury herself under an ugly bonnet and an ill-fitting dress, but she had once been a lady of quality, he would judge.

Well, at least she was not a timid, cringing creature. Clarissa would have rolled up such a woman in a day. No, Miss Midden had nerve and opinions. She was proud, in fact, and he knew enough about the world to suspect that that pride of hers had brought her to this lowly station. She probably had spurned the charity of relatives.

Ah, well, if he was reduced to idle speculation about a governess and her past, it was a sure sign he would make no more headway with his paperwork today. *Damn,* but it served him well that he had come home to such a tangle of papers. He had left his homecoming too long. However, the letter informing him of Phillip's death had found him just after Vitoria, and struggling to keep order in an army that wanted to loot the fallen city. He'd had no time then to think of going home, and with the push from Spain into France looming before the army, he had thought his duty lay with his men, not his family. So he had delayed through the autumn, and then into winter, when campaigning normally came to a halt. He'd gone to Wellington then, offering to stay on through the last battles against the French. But the Beau saw better where Andrew's duty lay, and told him to go home. It would all be over by that spring, Wellington had said.

And, indeed, to judge by the reports in the paper, the war soon would be ended.

Ah, but he'd rather be in France facing Soult than here facing these damn papers, and Dorothy and his duties. But duty was duty, and it was time to tell Dorothy that her precious child had been put into someone else's control.

He glanced at his desk and realized that Miss Midden had not taken with her the packet he had prepared. She had not wanted a year's salary. Well, she would have something to tempt her to stay. He pulled out a crisp ten-pound banknote, nearly two months' salary for her position. She might have a conscience, but women were practical at heart, after all. He also took up the schedule for her, for he was damn well going to establish some order in this household.

He knew he ought to summon a footman or a maid to take up the papers. But he had a desire to see what Miss Midden thought of her room, and if she was well settled. He had, after all, a strong interest in seeing her happily—and firmly—ensconced. It would be more difficult for her to remove herself from comfortable quarters. So he took himself up the stairs, his stride covering two carpeted steps at a time.

At the top, he took the left turning to the occupied wing, and since Miss Midden's door was open, he paused in the threshold, unexpectedly surprised.

Two

He had thought her taller. And not so attractive. The shock of just how attractive she looked lanced through him, sharp and startling for being so unexpected. Perhaps it was merely the size of the bedchamber that made her seem so small and slim. The room had been a state bedroom in the time of Charles I, and it still carried the baroque splendor of that era. In the grand room, with its rich blue hangings, Miss Midden seemed more a girl than a woman.

She stood with her back to the door, looking out the window onto the front lawn, the blue velvet curtains held back with one small, white hand. Her brown hair lay as smooth as a cap, pulled into a braided knot of some sort at the back, but stray wisps emphasized the slender elegance of her long neck. She had thrown off that wretched brown bonnet and it lay on the bed, sagging alongside her brown coat. He had a view of the back of an equally brown dress. The fabric shone with age and the seams looked ready to rip, given a deep enough breath, and he started to picture the sensual curve of shoulder and white skin that such a rip would offer up to his view.

Guilt for such thoughts flamed though him. He had no business speculating about an employee's form. He cleared his voice, and she turned, her mouth forming a small "O" of surprise. Her eyes lowered at once, but darted back up as if she could not contain her curiosity.

He held out the papers, feeling monumentally awkward. "You forgot these."

The words seemed abrupt to him, but did a lord apologize to a governess for intruding? His new protocols baffled him, for he was not about to copy his father's stiff and stilted manners.

As a younger son, he'd always been on easy terms with the servants. He had ignored the training given to Phillip, and in the army, rank was a thing easily grasped and automatically ordered. Since his homecoming, however, he had felt the watchful stares of the servants upon him, and had seen their expressions of disapproval and dismay. He was not doing things as Phillip had done them. *Damn* Phillip. *And damn me for being such a blockhead as to have never paid any mind to what a lord should or should not do.*

Miss Midden stepped across the room to take the packet, her booted feet light upon the carpet. She lowered her gaze again, but a slight smile turned up her lips. "Thank you. But I would have been pleased to come back down to see you, if you had sent someone to fetch me, my lord."

It was a small correction, and he wished suddenly that more of his household staff would give him such gracious guidance. He liked to know where he stood. But then, that sort of gentle correction was her stock-in-trade, was it not?

He folded his hands behind his back. "I wanted to make sure you were comfortable. The room—it will suit you? It's not too small?"

He knew it was not. The Blue Room with its painted ceiling and canopied bed had awed two hundred years of guests at Rothe House. It seemed that Miss Midden did not impress so easily. There was a knowing glint in her eyes that almost shouted, *I know you put me here to lure me into staying.*

"I shall be quite comfortable for a month or so," she said, giving him a firm look that said she would not change her mind.

Her eyes were actually gray-blue, he saw, not the brown he had thought them in his study. Another surprise. And the laughter lurking in them caught him off guard.

Not a pretty face, he thought, with its oval shape and unremarkable features. Nothing to tempt a man. But he liked her eyes. He liked Miss Midden, as well, he decided. She was forthright and strong-willed. Those traits would do splendidly for Clarissa. So how did he make up Miss Midden's mind for her that she was to stay?

"I thought you would prefer to have a room near Clarissa," he lied, and then added, without a qualm about another falsehood, "We are short of bedchambers. My grandfather had a habit of throwing his candle across the room to douse it, and one night his valet was not quick enough into the room to douse the bed curtains."

Miss Midden's lips thinned. Did she disapprove of his irreverent story about his grandfather? Then he caught the elusive glimmer in her eyes. Ah, she was not disapproving. She was trying to preserve propriety, for a smile would make her look less like a prim governess.

"How very unfortunate," she said, her voice soft. "Was the resulting fire large?"

"It carried off most of the west wing," he answered honestly. "My father never got around to rebuilding, and then my elder brother always meant to rebuild but never did."

"It seems a shame that you might break with such a family tradition by actually rebuilding, my lord."

Humor danced in her eyes, pulling an answering smile from him. "I am as poor at family traditions as I am unpracticed at being a lord. Address me as Lord Rothe or as my lord only if you wish to ensure I do not answer.

Colonel Derhurst, Derhurst, or a simple sir will suffice to get my attention, Miss Midden."

"A 'simple sir' is the last address I would give you . . . Colonel." She did smile this time, and then she opened the packet. Her eyes widened slightly at the ten-pound banknote and her fingers trembled, but the money seemed forgotten as she frowned over the schedule he'd drawn up for Clarissa's instruction.

"Is there something the matter?" he asked, making certain that his tone did not invite her to say "yes." He had perfected that tone with his aides and counted on it now to ensure her compliance.

"No . . . nothing," she began properly enough. Then she veered off his expectations by adding, "It is just . . . well, do you not think that perhaps this is a touch rigid for a girl of sixteen? I mean to say, an hour of French every day at ten o'clock . . ." She looked up at him. "What if on a particularly fine day we wish to do an hour of botany in the gardens instead of French? Unexpected events do happen—with girls of sixteen, that is."

Andrew felt the line between his eyebrows tighten. "Clarissa needs discipline. She needs structure. There has been no order in her life since her father died last June, and her mother spoils her with an unseemly amount of freedom."

"I don't wish to be impertinent, but unseemly by what standards?"

"For someone who does not wish to be impertinent, you are near to doing just that," he shot back, scowling at her and beginning to reconsider the many virtues of Miss Midden.

"I beg your pardon. It is just that what is unseemly in a mature woman must be overlooked in a child as a habit that will soon pass. If Clarissa is child enough to still warrant a governess, then you must not judge her by the standards society sets for a grown woman."

"You argue against your own earlier excuse that Clarissa is too old for a governess."

"Ah, you are right. And in that case, this schedule will not do at all, for it is a schedule suitable for a child. So if I may, I will adapt your hours to better occupy a young lady. I have great experience with young ladies of sixteen and seventeen, so I am certain you must wish to leave me some room to apply my expertise."

Andrew's brow now hurt from frowning so hard. Somehow, he had been outflanked, and there was nothing for it but to retreat, regroup and count his losses later. To do otherwise would only make him look ridiculous—and he knew damn well that that was not suitable for a lord.

"Yes . . . well . . . I shall leave you to make your schedules and present them to me. But I must insist upon some regular hours. And I should introduce you to Dorothy—Lady Rothe, Clarissa's mother. She will not like you, but you need not let that bother you in any fashion."

"She has already made up her mind against me?" Miss Midden asked. She turned away so that he could not see her face to see if any worry lay behind her cautious words. She folded her banknote—she was keeping the bribe, he noted with satisfaction—and his schedule and placed them in her reticule on the dresser.

As he started down the hall with her, he explained, "My sister-in-law dotes on her dogs and on her daughter, whom she believes is already a perfect paragon. She does not take well to interference."

"Well, perhaps then it would be best to introduce me as a paid companion."

She said this in such a reasonable voice that for a moment he was tempted to go along with her proposal. However, it seemed far too like a concession in the silent battle of wills that he had started with his late brother's wife.

When he had returned home last month, he had requested a doctor to call up on Lady Rothe. There was nothing physically wrong with her, so he had requested that she attend to her duties and her daughter. Lady Rothe accused him of being heartless. He accused her of having grown lazy. That interview—and three others in succession—ended with Lady Rothe in tears and him slamming out of the room to ride off his ill humor.

But he was not going to cave in to Dorothy's passive warfare. It had taken him too long to end his military obligations and take up his duties at home. However, he was damned if he would allow Dorothy to punish him for that. Nor was he going to allow her laziness to ruin his niece.

As they approached Lady Rothe's chambers, Miss Midden paused and laid a soft hand on his arm. "Please, Colonel. It would make my time here far more productive if I began on a good footing with Lady Rothe."

She had very small hands and she wore no ornament, save for one gold ring on her littlest finger. She wore no perfume; only the clean smell of soap adorned her. He frowned, but he did not wish to lose his governess on her first day of hire.

"Very well. If that is what you wish. But I warn you, I will make it clear that you are to have charge of Clarissa."

Miss Midden nodded, her eyes downcast again, and he wished she would look up so that he might have a glimpse into her eyes and into what she was thinking. He distrusted her acquiescence. He suspected that too much went on in that quick mind of hers for it to bend so easily to the will of others.

Then he turned and opened the door to Lady Rothe's rooms.

Three

Maeve settled one hand over her stomach to control her nervousness. It was silly, this desire to have Lady Rothe like her. She would be here only a month, perhaps six weeks at most, as agreed upon with the colonel—Lord Rothe, she reminded herself, though she found it as difficult as he to think of him as a lord. Still, she did not look forward to being employed in a household where she might be actively disliked.

Looking about her, Maeve tried to gain some sense of the mistress from the surroundings.

The bedchamber she had followed the colonel into was large, and everywhere she looked there seemed to be some carved ornament or plaster cherub. It was rather like stepping into a gilt-edged meringue—all white spoony curves and too sweet for her taste.

Then she saw Lady Rothe.

Propped up by pillows, Lady Rothe sat upon a large bed at the opposite end of the room. She, too, seemed all fussy white lace and flounces and curves. Her face was round and pink as a child's, her ample curves smoothing out any hint of wrinkles. It was difficult to set her age, but she seemed far too young to be confined to her bed by infirmity. Gold curls peeked out from a frivolous lace cap, and large blue eyes regarded the colonel and Maeve with a wary petulance, as if Lady Rothe expected an unpleasant scene and was already bracing for it. Books lay scattered about her like a child's playthings.

Beside her ladyship three black and white King Charles spaniels sprawled on the bed, their pink tongues dangling, their bulging dark eyes echoing the guarded belligerence of their mistress. The dogs began to growl as the colonel approached.

"Hush, Conrad. Manfred . . . quiet. No, sit down, Theo. Stay, all of you," Lady Rothe said, laying down her book upon the bed. The dogs began to resettle, pushing books out of their way for a cushioned spot, and Lady Rothe turned her stare back to the intruders.

That forceful glare held a glint which reminded Maeve strongly of Clarissa's willful gaze, and Maeve's nerve began to falter. This was no fretting invalid, but a woman who looked unhappy and capable of making a very uncomfortable scene.

Maeve glanced up at the colonel, hoping that by some amazing miracle he might have changed his mind about hiring her. However, he looked grimly determined, his eyes narrowed, his jaw set. Her stomach knotted again. Oh, dear, indeed.

The colonel folded his hands behind his back. "Dorothy, this is Clarissa's new . . ."

Please do not say governess, Maeve silently prayed.

". . . companion," the colonel finished, hesitating an instant over the word.

Maeve hid a smile. She would have to find some way to thank the colonel for that small concession, but not by staying on. Not if Lady Rothe was so set against anyone interfering with her daughter's upbringing.

"Companion?" Lady Rothe said, her tone echoed by a dog's low growl. "Oh, hush now, Theo," she commanded, then turned back to the colonel, peering at him as if she needed spectacles. "A companion for Clarissa? But there are nearly half a dozen girls in the neighborhood who are near to her age, and she can readily visit with any of them." Lady Rothe's eyes widened. "She is a governess, isn't she? You ignored my express wishes and have hired a governess for my little darling." Tears began to well in the large blue eyes. "It is not enough that I lost Phillip. Now you mean to take my darling angel from me!"

The dogs rumbled as Lady Rothe fumbled for a handkerchief. Her search disturbed the blackest of the trio—Theo or Conrad or Manfred, Maeve could not tell which, and the spaniel jumped up, knocking Lady Rothe's book to the floor.

Maeve moved without thought, bending down to pick up the leather-bound work.

"I have told you, Dorothy—" the colonel began.

Lady Rothe let out an even larger sob.

Maeve glanced from one to the other. A sense of guilt stung her that while this argument was none of her making, it was very much centered squarely on her presence here. She had some responsibility to smooth matters as much as she could. Only how was she to do so without making an enemy of one or the other?

She glanced down at the book in her hands and found sudden inspiration.

"Oh, you are reading *Marmion*," Maeve said, staring at the leather binding and not daring to look up. She could feel the stares of the potential combatants hot upon her skin, and if she looked up now she would forget her courage. So she babbled on. "Sir Walter is quite one of my favorites. I adored *Lady of the Lake*, and I hear he is to have a new work out this year."

"Wherever did you hear such a thing?" Lady Rothe demanded, her tone suspicious, as if no one of Maeve's insignificance could ever hear anything important. But Maeve caught one weak shade of curiosity in her ladyship's tone.

She glanced up to confide, "Well, Mrs. Durbin, my

last employer, she kept a correspondence with Mrs. Armitage, who lives in London and who has an acquaintance with Miss Fanny Burney—"

"Not *the* Fanny Burney . . . the authoress?" Lady Rothe asked, astonished reverence thickening her voice.

"The very one. And Miss Burney wrote to Mrs. Armitage who passed the news on to Mrs. Durbin who told me that Mr. Scott had delivered a new work to his publisher and it was his best yet."

"Oh, my, what wonderful news. Oh, you must come and sit down here with me, child, and tell me more. Theo, do stop growling. You must not mind Theo. She is always cross when she is woken from her naps. Oh, go away, Andrew. Do you not see we have much to discuss here. What did you say your name was?"

"This is Miss Maeve Midden," the colonel said, picking up as if he had not been interrupted. He planted his booted feet wide and looked not the least inclined to "go away" as he had been bidden. "And I did not hire her to be your companion, Dorothy."

"No, of course, not," Maeve said, stepping forward. "But it is quite understandable that Lady Rothe would wish to speak to me, to ensure I share her sensibilities and views. Is that not so, my lady?"

"Oh, yes, yes, but tell me, did you not adore *Camilla* by Miss Burney? I cried positive rivers when I read it . . . oh, it must be years ago. It is still quite one of my favorites."

"You must also favor Mr. Walpole's *Castle of Otranto* to have named your dogs for his characters," Maeve said, sitting on the edge of a chair that was positioned near the bed.

With that, the two women began to chatter about books read, comparing gothic novels, conversing like true blood-sisters of the inked tale. Colonel Derhurst listened to them, baffled and frustrated. He thought once about interrupting, but as he fidgeted, Miss Midden shot him a look that stopped his words upon his tongue.

It was a look that conveyed many messages, and the odd thing was that he understood every one of them far better than he understood the ramble of authors and book titles tumbling from her lips. That look of hers held a plea, an offer of gratitude for his silence, and an edge of warning that she was well in command and he had best stay out of it. All of that came from those gray-blue eyes in just a flash, a frown and a lifted eyebrow. He responded to it with a silence that came mostly from astonishment that she could convey so very much in such an economical fashion.

So he tugged on his watch fob and listened to the ladies agree to dislike Byron—poetry, Lady Roth declared, made her head ache with its rhymes. And he began to think well of Miss Midden's handling of the matter. Dorothy had not yet broken into angry sobs.

Finally, Miss Midden rose. "But I have kept you too long from your story, my lady."

"Dorothy. You must call me Dorothy. It is almost more than I can bear to hear my title, for it reminds me of my recent loss." Her eyes began to tear again with amazing ease.

Maeve heard a grinding sound and glanced over to see the colonel's jaw tense. It was his teeth grating, she realized. She smoothed her skirts, wishing they were made of something stiff so they might rustle and cover the colonel's impatience with her ladyship's display of excessive sensibility.

"I am so very sorry for your loss . . . you must be terribly lonely," Maeve said, handing back the book to her ladyship.

"Thank you, my dear." Dorothy looked up and over her handkerchief and fixed a haughty stare on the colonel.

"There are those who have no understanding when it comes to matters of the heart."

"And what a blessing that is," the colonel muttered.

Dorothy's face flushed, and Maeve interrupted before a new battle began. "Colonel, perhaps you could take me to talk with Clarissa now?"

"Yes, Andrew, take our dear Maeve to meet Clarissa. But you must come back to sit with me after dinner tonight, my dear. I always take dinner in my rooms, for my constitution has not been robust since my . . . since I lost my dear, dear husband."

Maeve caught the vexed spark in the colonel's eyes, and hurriedly said, "I shall be happy to come, and I will bring Clarissa with me as well."

And he cannot object to that, Maeve decided, for if she knew anything about men, then she knew he was a man who would enjoy an evening with his paper and little other company.

Maeve started for the door at once, hoping to make a graceful end to this interview. The dogs set to yapping again, and as the door closed behind them, Maeve could still hear her ladyship hushing the animals.

"Your skills extend to wider age range than I expected, Miss Midden," the colonel remarked dryly as he led the way down the hall. "But while I will not argue with your tactics—not after seeing you so handily win that skirmish—I hope you will keep in mind that your primary object is to deal with Clarissa, not her mother."

Maeve stopped and turned toward him, irritated. "I am glad you do not want to argue, but I could wish that you might refrain from thinking of those around you in terms of battle and offense and defense. It does rather sound as if you regard your own family more in the nature of enemies to be subjugated, instead of loving relations."

She did not expect him to smile, but he did. It swept

her irritation out from her like a wave knocking her feet from underneath her.

"You may save your instruction for Clarissa, Miss Midden. She is in grave need of it, while I am long past mending my ways," he said, striding ahead to lead the way.

Maeve could only meekly follow, and wonder if the colonel was right not only about his niece's need for guidance, but about his own lack of need.

It turned out that Maeve did not get an immediate formal introduction to Clarissa. Now she was wanted, the girl could not be found. She was not waiting in her room as ordered, a fact which brought the set look back to the colonel's mouth. The reprieve left Maeve with time to rest and change before dinner. Rothe House kept country hours, meaning that dinner came early, at five.

Unpacking and folding her clothes into the large mahogany wardrobe, Maeve realized how very little space her possessions took up. She had one good dress, a black bombazine for Sunday, her schoolroom dress which was a soft gray and could withstand the markings of chalk wiped from slate boards, her brown traveling dress, and a much faded blue walking dress. With two petticoats, a nightgown and a few unmentionables, her entire range of clothing took up less than half the wardrobe's space.

She could remember a time when she'd had a new dress every week—but that was a lifetime ago.

She put aside such memories and left to ask the housekeeper, Mrs. Henderson, about a pressing for her brown dress. After some debate, she had decided that dinner did not quite warrant her black dress. She found Mrs. Henderson a nervous, thin woman, but friendly and kind. That was a stronger lure to stay than even the money had been, for it had been years since she had received such consideration.

However, staring at her reflection in the mirror before dinner, and running her hands down her newly pressed dress, Maeve firmly told herself, "You will keep the future in mind, for once, miss. For this is the ideal time to find a house with six girls in it, all under age eight."

She nodded at her reflection, trying to be cheered by what she saw. She had never been pretty, and the years had taken away much of youth's dewy grace. Her skin— her one vanity—lay smooth and white as it had when she was nineteen. But she was twenty-eight now. Her cheeks were hollow, not plump and rosy, and the shadows under her eyes grew darker every year. She pinched her cheeks to give them some color and then left her room in search of Clarissa.

She hoped for a few words in private with the girl. She wanted to put to rest any notion that she was here as that much-dreaded commodity—a governess. However, the colonel was already downstairs in the drawing room which the footman had indicated, and Clarissa was with him, looking defiant but cowed.

That man had a rare talent for putting women into a temper, Maeve decided after glancing from Clarissa's trembling lips to the colonel's grim face, and she silently wished his military promptness to perdition.

Clarissa came forward, her manners dutiful, but her blue eyes held dangerous glints of fire.

Sixteen and wishing she were twenty-two, and beautiful in the bargain, Maeve decided. A combination that could easily make for disaster. She knew that all too well from her own experience—and she had not even been beautiful. Only willful.

"How do you do?" Clarissa said, pronouncing each word with a rehearsed clarity. "I understand you are to instruct me in deportment, manners and becoming conduct."

Maeve guessed that the colonel had put those words into the girl's mouth. *Oh, bother the man. Why had he said all that to the child?*

Maeve put on a smile and folded her hands in front of her. "Did he also tell you that I am to stay only a month or so? In that time, I hope I may offer you my friendship, and what knowledge I have of the world is at your disposal. But you are too old for a governess and you have a mother, so perhaps I may be something in between?"

With a lift of her pointed chin, Clarissa shot an indignant look at the colonel. "You didn't say she was not to stay."

"The duration of Miss Midden's employment is something for me and Miss Midden to decide. You may concern yourself with learning to behave."

Thankfully, the butler came to announce dinner, and Clarissa had to swallow whatever retort simmered inside her.

The colonel offered his arm to Miss Midden, who would rather have avoided that honor, but she was the eldest woman in the room, even if she was only an employee and not a guest. She placed her hand on his sleeve, noting that it was rather pleasant to walk into a dining room on a man's arm, particularly such a firm arm.

Blushing at her thoughts, she lowered her stare to her plate and kept it there.

Dinner slipped past with conversation that was as bland as the food. The lack of spoken exchange did not surprise Maeve, not with Clarissa threatening sulks and the colonel ignoring his niece. But Mrs. Henderson had seemed a competent housekeeper, so why did she put up with such poor fare from the cook? Maeve spent the meal speculating on whether the plain food could be credited to the colonel's preferences, or to a kitchen trying to cater to the invalidish Lady Rothe.

After the last course was removed, Miss Midden rose. "Will you join us directly, Colonel?"

"I never touch port, but I will stay to blow a cloud . . . it's a habit my niece does not care for."

Clarissa wrinkled her nose, which seemed to amuse the colonel. "It does not suit my niece's idea of a lord, but I am not about to give up my cigarillo after dinner to fit her notions."

"Then we shall leave you to your smoke," Maeve said, and left with Clarissa.

The girl said nothing until they were seated in the drawing room where Maeve had first met Clarissa that afternoon. It had grown dark outside, but a merry fire in the carved fireplace and several dozen candles warmed the room.

Maeve glanced around, admiring the paintings on the walls—one particularly fine one of a horse. She needed some gambit to draw Clarissa into regarding her as something other than a ball and chain. She noticed the pianoforte in the far corner of the room, and so she asked, indicating it, "Do you play, Clarissa?"

"A little," the girl answered, her voice indifferent. Then she glanced at Maeve from the corners of her eyes.

Maeve guessed at once that the girl was waiting to see if a reprimand would come for such a curt answer, but she was not about to be goaded into making the mistake of presuming to correct Clarissa. She waited, wondering if her silence would urge the girl's conscience do the rest.

Clarissa fidgeted with the ribbons on her dress, then added, "My uncle does not seem to like it when I play. And I cannot blame him, for the pianoforte never seems to hold a tuning. I think the damp got into it this past winter."

Maeve smiled. Clarissa had proven she at least had some sense of decorum.

The fire crackled, emphasizing the silence in the room.

Maeve sat for a moment, staring at the leaping flames. Their warmth was welcome, for the spring nights grew chill after the sun had set. Perhaps she should bring up the weather as a suitable topic to discuss? Or the history of the house . . . or the furniture?

"Did you know that I am named after Mr. Samuel Richardson's heroine Clarissa Harlow?"

Maeve looked up to study the girl. She sensed a test behind this odd, graceless question. Would Clarissa dismiss any reply which failed to demonstrate an understanding of why she had launched this particular conversational gambit?

"Really?" Maeve said, stalling for time and realizing that Clarissa was not quite the spoilt, empty-headed child she seemed. There was direction and planning behind this question, and while Clarissa might be a handful, there was need behind her misbehavior.

Maeve ransacked her memory for any details of the book, but she could only remember it as an unpleasant tale of a girl seduced to her doom by a charming man.

"I do not recall the particulars," Maeve said, striving for honesty. "But I seem to remember Mr. Richardson's Clarissa as rather silly. Did she not pine away or some such thing?"

Clarissa frowned and gave an impatient and childish shrug, and Maeve wondered if she had said the right thing. But then Clarissa said, her tone worldly beyond her years, "She starved herself to death. Over a man. I should never do that."

Maeve resisted the urge to smile at the contrast between Clarissa's attempt at bored sophistication and her still childish face. "A wise choice."

"But she did have adventures," Clarissa went on. "And she was rather fearless to act as she did. Only she ought to have married Lovelace, you know. He begged her to.

And my godmama who lives in London swears that a reformed rake always makes the best husband."

Maeve decided that Clarissa's godmama had no business putting such utter nonsense into this girl's head. She did not wish to spoil Clarissa's charming innocence, but too much of that commodity led only to ruination.

She fixed a firm stare on the girl. "Actually, rakes are generally selfish men who really should never marry. And I have found that it is difficult enough to reform one's own character without trying to take on the improvement of someone else."

Clarissa's eyes took on a challenging glitter. "But are you not here to improve me? To remake my character?"

Ah, so that is where we are heading, Maeve thought, relaxing. "I have it on your uncle's authority that your mother believes you to be perfection. How could I improve upon that? And that brings to mind a request from your mother that we visit with her this evening. Perhaps read with her a bit."

With a huge sigh, Clarissa slumped against the couch, looking less like a young lady of uncertain temper and more like an unhappy child. "But I read with mother every night."

Maeve heard in the girl's voice the desperate plea of the young for new horizons. Sympathy tangled with her resolve to maintain her emotional distance. She was not staying. It really was none of her concern.

"I am certain she appreciates it," she said.

Clarissa gave another deep sigh. "Perhaps. But she doesn't love me. Not the way she loved my father. No one cares about me. I am nothing but a pawn to be used by her . . . and by my uncle."

This statement left Maeve floundering between amusement at such theatrics and shock that Clarissa could confess any such thing to a near stranger.

"I am certain that is not so. Your mother's sole concern

is your well-being, and as for your uncle . . . well, you are his brother's only child. How could he not care for you?"

The girl glanced behind her to the doorway, and an uncomfortable sensation chased along Maeve's spine— the sensation of having stepped into a puddle and not yet found the bottom with her foot.

"Ah, but you don't understand," Clarissa said, her voice lowering dramatically, "My mother was once in love with both the Derhurst brothers. She broke Uncle Andrew's heart when she chose to marry his brother. My uncle fled into the army. Now he uses me to punish her. And he hates me because I remind him of the woman he loved and can never have, for it is immoral for a man to marry his brother's widow."

Maeve tried to think of some answer to give to this . . . this romantic exaggeration. Then the door to the drawing room opened and the colonel stepped in.

He looked as dark as a phantom in his evening clothes, his expression abstracted, and with such a bleak look in his dark eyes that Maeve's heart gave out a small cry of recognition for someone else who has known deep suffering.

Oh, dear, could Clarissa possibly be right about him?

Four

The colonel glanced up, his remote mood vanishing, replaced by a frown that Maeve was beginning to think was more a habit than any indicator of his true mood. He seemed always to look as if he were concentrating on strategy and tactics and the next battle to be fought.

He came into the room, his step brisk. A faint but not unpleasant smell of tobacco clung to his clothes. "Good evening, ladies. I trust I did not keep you waiting. Have you rung for tea yet, Clarissa?"

"Are you certain you would not rather send me to bed with warm milk and my nanny?" Clarissa shot back, the militant glint coming back into her eyes.

"Actually, I have always preferred a glass of milk before bed," Maeve said, interrupting before Clarissa dug herself too deep a grave. "Isn't it odd that growing older so often means that one is required to give up the small comforts of life?"

Both the colonel and Clarissa turned to stare at Maeve as if she had suddenly spouted a third arm. Maeve felt the color rise to her cheeks, but her distraction had served its purpose in disarming the combatants.

"And speaking of comforts, I believe, Colonel, that we are promised to Lady Rothe for tea."

Maeve rose. She was not quite certain that she believed Clarissa's exaggerated story of revenge and lost love. However, she knew that this was indeed a troubled household. But her obligation was simply to provide companionship to Clarissa . . . and perhaps a little guidance as well. She would have to ignore this growing desire to do something for these people. Had she not just offered Clarissa excellent advice on not attempting to reform the characters of others?

She must remember to perform her duties with a cool detachment appropriate to her situation. She was not going to wear her heart on her sleeve so that it could be torn apart yet again when the inevitable parting came.

"If you will excuse us, Colonel, we will say our good nights here and keep Lady Rothe company for a short time before retiring."

She gave a small curtsy to the colonel and then looked expectantly at Clarissa. The girl rose, seemed to debate for a moment on how civil she would be to her uncle, and then copied Maeve's example, dropping a short curtsy.

The colonel went to open the door for them. Maeve allowed Clarissa to leave and then, just before she stepped out, the colonel put two fingers on her arm, making her pause.

"Well, you see now what there is to deal with. Clarissa may well be spoilt beyond redemption. Perhaps you are wise to look elsewhere, Miss Midden, for a less daunting charge, but I still hope to persuade you to take up this challenge."

Maeve swallowed the dryness in her throat. She looked down, away from the smile that had softened his expression and which curved attractively on his lips. "You are a determined man."

"Is that such a bad thing, Miss Midden?"

She glanced up at him. He was not smiling, but amusement lurked in his eyes, and so she grew bold. "I have known men so determined upon a course that the cost to others never came into account. Determination can be an admirable trait, so long as it is not someone's only trait."

His eyebrows rose, and for a moment irritation tightened his mouth. He was not a man accustomed to being taken to task, Maeve realized. But she stood her ground. If he dismissed her on the spot, she would be no worse off than she had been the day before coming to this house. Indeed, she would be freed of what looked to be a most uncomfortable month here.

But then he smiled again. "You sound as if you speak from experience, Miss Midden. And it is perhaps an apt lesson for both your pupils, I think. Good night, then. I trust you will sleep well at Rothe House."

He bowed her out of the room, and she left, thinking him a very uncomfortable man. And far too perceptive.

Was he really still in love with his late brother's wife?

Over the next few days, Maeve's life took on a new pattern, and the questions she had about Lord Rothe—the colonel—returned to haunt her. She saw little of him, other than for a short time each evening at dinner and just after. All too often, Clarissa occupied his attention by antagonizing him. Maeve recognized the signs of a girl who wanted—needed—a father's attention but could not have it. But the colonel seemed blind to Clarissa's stumbling efforts to make him notice her, even if that came in the form of an argument.

Maeve was thinking of this—and what to do about it— as she came down to breakfast. Mornings had become luxuriously her own. Lady Rothe seemed to be confined to her room by whatever ailment she suffered, and Clarissa chose to take breakfast in her room as well. The colonel rose at some ungodly hour, and evidence of his having breakfasted lightly always greeted Maeve in the breakfast room.

Maeve liked the room with its yellow walls and bright morning light. And she gave thanks that she could drink her tea in solitude. She had never been at her best in the mornings, and it took her a full hour to shake off both lethargy and a mood that bordered on surly until she had had her morning pot of tea.

This morning, Maeve drank her tea and thought about the day ahead. She had already finished her letter of application to Mr. Jessup for a new position, and she had nothing to do but wait for Clarissa to come downstairs. That, she had learned, could take some time. So she decided she might as well pass the time with a walk in the garden. It was a pity, after all, not to take advantage of a spring day that dawned without rain.

After a trip upstairs to fetch a light shawl against any winter breeze still stirring, Maeve stepped outside. She left her bonnet behind, preferring to have the sun warm her cheeks. She never freckled, thankfully.

The air carried a sharp bite, a reminder that spring had only officially arrived just a few days ago. Around her, gardeners dug at weeds and trimmed hedges, and everywhere there seemed the promise of blossoms to come. A moment's temptation stirred in Maeve. She wiggled her toes in her shoes. How lovely it would be to stroll barefoot in the grass, letting the cool blades tickle her toes, the ground soft and warm under her feet. However, with so many gardeners around, and maids hurrying in and out as they went about their duties, she would have to be proper and keep her shoes on her feet.

She stayed on the terrace and made herself be content with admiring the daffodils that now stood at attention like army buglers, their trumpets just starting to open and flare. The thought left her smiling. She was turning as military-minded as the colonel.

Then she rounded the corner of the building and her

step faltered. Speak of the devil and he shall appear, and here he was indeed.

Lord Rothe stood with his back to her, hatless, a strong, dark shape against the green of the grass and the white stone of the west wing of the house.

He stood a head taller than the man with him, and the two seemed to be discussing an unruly set of plans that the breeze pulled at and flapped. Behind them, the top-floor of the west wing had windows empty of any frames or glass. The wing was roofless and sightless, like a blind, injured thing. It looked so bleak that she gratefully turned her attention to his lordship.

His black hair gave off a faint blue sheen in the sunlight. But even if he had worn a hat, she could not have mistaken him. He had perhaps the best set of shoulders she had ever seen on a man. The strong width of them tapered along a graceful sweep of back. He was built well for a tall man, for there was nothing bulky or lumbering about him. Instead, his lean figure commanded her attention and her admiration, sending a warm flush along her skin and inspiring thoughts most unsuitable to a governess.

Still, what harm was there in looking? So she paused on the terrace, her shawl pulled tight, and enjoyed the view and wished that just once she could smooth the palm of her hand across the sinew and bone of that man's shoulders.

A small sigh slipped out of her lips. She pulled her shoulders back and tried to also pull back her wandering wits.

She decided she should not linger, but she was still standing there when he turned suddenly, his eyes narrowed. She blushed hot as a schoolgirl caught in the act and hesitated. That proved her greatest mistake, for he started toward her, and now she could not simply turn about and run away like the coward she was. She hoped devoutly that her red cheeks could be mistaken for being wind-blown.

Andrew covered the distance between himself and Miss Midden in a dozen strides. He had been aware of her standing there and watching for the past few minutes, but he had been in the middle of telling Shandwick, the builder, some of his ideas for the improvements he wanted done with the ruined wing. Shandwick was being his usual obstinate Yorkshire self. While he did not flatly refuse to do the work, his answer to each request came with a sullen, "Aye, if you want it that way." That way, of course, being implicitly the wrong way.

It was a relief to dismiss Mr. Shandwick and exchange his company for that of Miss Midden. She might have as many opinions as Shandwick, but at least she did not turn sullen. God save him from women who sulked to get what they wanted.

"You look well, Miss Midden," he said after bidding her good morning. "More color in your face. Our Northern climate must agree with you."

Her cheeks reddened further until they shone like ripe apples. She dropped her gaze to his boots. *Damn,* but he probably should not have complimented a governess. Only it was the truth. She did look well with color on her cheeks. Her face was usually too pale.

"What do you think of our ruin?" he asked, keeping his tone bluff and folding his hands behind his back. He wanted to take her arm so that she must walk with him, but she might feel awkward at such presumption. "Do you care to take a closer look? The rotten wood's been carted off, so what's left is sound enough, if none too pretty."

"I am not certain I should take the time. Clarissa will be up and about soon." She glanced up at him, her eyes sparking mischievously. "And we have French at ten, according to your schedule."

"*My* schedule, is it? I will not allow you to use that excuse, for you have already insisted on a release from my tyranny. And I have a much better excuse to need your company, for I'm trying to put as much time between me and when I must meet with my steward. He insisted on discussing drainage today, and I fear it is yet another subject about which I will show an embarrassing amount of ignorance."

She tilted her head and studied him, looking rather like an inquisitive sparrow. "You could just tell him to do as he thinks best."

"And have him think me such a poor commander that I lay my plans without any knowledge of the territory around me? No, learning about pasture drains is my duty today, but I shall have some pleasure first by showing you around a more enjoyable project."

He took her hand into the small of his arm. If it was not protocol to do so, it was at least good manners. She was such a tiny thing, and her hand lay passive on his arm, as delicate as fine porcelain. He suspected that, like bone china, a deceptive strength lay under that delicate form. He could see the resolution in her eyes, and he could sense it in how she carried herself. Whatever hardships had brought her to Rothe House had acted like a kiln's fire on her, hardening her to the core.

She was a kindred soul. He knew that without needing to know anything else, and it was a pleasure he hugged close inside himself that he had found in her a fellow warrior of life.

She fell into step beside him, finding that the grass was a more fascinating view than he was. "When do you begin to rebuild?"

"This summer. I want the rains well over before we lay any fresh framing."

The necessity of opening doors and climbing the stairs to the ruined floors in the west wing prevented any further conversation, but when they emerged on the second floor, he had the pleasure of seeing her face alight with interest and awe.

It was a sight that should inspire both.

The upper story of the wing had burnt down to its stone foundations. Woodwork, furnishings, fittings all had been ruined and had been stripped away, leaving a vast open space that stretched from the front of the house to the back, with its stone floor and roofless stone walls. Overhead, the sky glowed softly blue.

The front looked out to the green lawns and home farm. At the back, empty windows showed the craggy hills that towered behind Rothe House. Maeve had glimpsed these hills yesterday, with their sharp, stony cliffs. They loomed up almost as if someone had cut off part of the mountainside, leaving this as a deep scar. But, framed by the stone windows, the hills seemed not so menacing. Now they simply looked wild and strong.

"It's . . . it's marvelous," Maeve said, drawn to the view at the back. "I've never seen rocks rise up so steeply."

"That is the Gordale Scar. Some say the overhanging rocks resemble monsters waiting to pounce. I always thought they looked more like rows and rows of soldiers. You can hike into the gorge, and there's a waterfall—the Gordale Beck. It can sound like thunder after a heavy rain."

She smiled back at him and strode across the room, her boots echoing on the stone floor as she walked over to a stone fireplace large enough to hold a roasting ox, the only adornment in the space. She turned once around. "It's so peaceful. You could almost imagine yourself in another world here. How can you bear to build it up again?"

His face relaxed into a smile, and Maeve felt again that small shiver of pleasure in having that focused charm of

his given to her. But she knew better than to make anything of it. That charm was not specific to her. He smiled
because he was amused by something; he did not smile
because of her, and she had to keep that in mind.

She looked over at the fireplace and studied the flowers
carved into the white limestone. She would do well to
emulate their composed, unchanging nature. But she
could not keep from hearing the colonel's firm step close
the distance to her, and she could not deny the awareness
of him as he stood beside her.

"There is a stark beauty here . . . in the room and outside it. But it is not a very useful area. I would like to
add new bedchambers—ones fitted with indoor plumb-
ing, if I can convince Mr. Shandwick to build them. He
seems to think that privy closets were good enough for
the last five generations of Derhursts, and so should be
good enough for the next five."

She smiled and darted a glance up at him. "How daring
of you to break with tradition. And will you take as your
room one to the back of the house with a view of the
Gordale Scar?"

"I can hardly see Dorothy or Clarissa wishing to wake
every morning to see those steep rocks rise up from the
river and grass and mists."

"I should adore it," Maeve said, then realized she
should not be talking about waking up in his bedchamber.
She swiftly veered off to more practical matters. "But I
hope you will not want to add the new gas lighting, such
as I have read has been installed on Westminster Bridge.
I do not believe they are safe."

"I would have thought that a practical woman such as
yourself would welcome such innovations. Would you
rather not have bright light to work by in an evening?"

"My lord, working longer hours is not a goal that any
governess, or companion, aspires to."

"What is it that a governess, or companion, aspires to?"

She glanced up at him. He stood with his arms folded, his face relaxed, his dark eyes amused. "Why, retirement, of course," she answered, her tone only half teasing. "With a decent pension after a long career at a household where I've had the joy of seeing the daughters of the house well established."

And that is exactly what I am going to find, she told herself, and then she told it to herself again in case he teased her into forgetting it.

"I would like to oblige you by offering you a position here until you retire, but I think Clarissa would definitely balk at having a governess—or a companion, for that matter—for another, what would it be, forty years or so?"

She laughed, thankful that he had turned the subject so neatly into a joke between them. "Thank you for that roundabout compliment, but I think I will be quite in my dotage in thirty years, not forty. And Clarissa will be in her dotage before she learns any French if I do not return to see if I can interest her in the subject."

They started back toward the main house.

To Maeve, the decorated rooms seemed cluttered after the stark simplicity of the ruined wing. She walked beside the colonel, following as he led her back to the bustle and noise of the rest of the house with its maids and footmen and busy staff.

"So you are trying to interest Clarissa in French? You seem to know your tactics, so I'll allow you to proceed as you like, but I will offer the comment that I strongly think that what Clarissa needs most is to learn how to take a direct order and obey it. She has no discipline."

Maeve stopped to face him. "How long were you in the army, Colonel?"

"Long enough that I'm marked for life by military hab-

its, its stiff carriage and poor manners. Do you imply I
was perhaps too long in service?" he asked, his eyes
warm and gleaming.

"I think you share your niece's desire to always tempt
me into unwise comments, so I shall not make an answer
to that."

"Then I shall make a firm answer to your question. I
ate the King's salt for eighteen years, ten months and five
days."

"Eighteen years? You must have joined very young."

"Now you are flattering me. My mirror—and my
valet—swear I look every one of my seven and thirty
years. I am well on my way to becoming one of those
doddering ancients, with hoary whiskers and endless bor-
ing war stories, or at least that is Clarissa's opinion."

Maeve heard the slight wistful tone in his voice, and
her fingers clenched around her shawl as she thought
about how cruel the young could be to their elders. If
only Clarissa would show a touch more kindness to her
uncle . . . and if only he would show a touch more patience.

She spoke none of these thoughts, but said, "I think
you would look quite distinguished with whiskers."

He glanced down at her, the barest trace of a smile
softening the hard lines of his mouth. "Then I shall en-
deavor to grow a set."

Maeve felt the heat tingle on her cheeks, but she went
on, her tone conversational, "After so long in the army,
I see how it might take some time to change your habits.
But I must ask you, Colonel, to please try to make a
change. Ordering Clarissa about is an excellent way to
encourage rebellion in her, not obedience. She is struggling to be an adult, and she believes she cannot become
one if she is treated like a child."

"I should be happy to treat her as an adult, if she were
to act as one. But I cannot . . ." He broke off and stood

staring off into space, his face set again. "I have a duty to my brother to do all that I can to see that Clarissa is well established. With any luck, I hope that day may come soon, but I cannot turn that girl loose on the world without first having some confidence that she can behave as a lady should."

She had put his back up with her slight criticism. She watched him, noting the precision with which he dressed—the neatly tied cravat, the well-placed gold pin in its white folds. He was an orderly man, a man who took pride in being exact. He would not like to be told he was doing something wrong.

He had folded his hands behind his back and looked as if he was trying to frame a more thoughtful response. Finally, he said, his voice low and almost reluctant, "Miss Midden, I bow to your experience in this matter and I will try to do what I can. But I make no promises. Just as you must act according to your conscience, so must I."

She smiled, relieved. It was not easy for such a man to bend, but he had just shown that he might be able to yield a tiny amount. Perhaps it would be enough—but that depended on Clarissa as well. Maeve's shoulders felt burdened suddenly with the responsibility for Clarissa that she had taken on. Oh, why had she not kept out of this? But she must do something for the girl while she was here.

"Thank you, my lord . . . Colonel. And I shall now take advantage of your kind mood to ask one more favor of you. Are there any ladies' fashion magazines in the house?"

"Fashion?" His eyes warmed with humor. "I hope this is a sign you are looking to replace this brown dress of yours, Miss Midden. Forgive me for saying so, but there are times I wonder if a deep breath will result in a broad display of your back."

Shannon Donnelly

She flushed red up to the roots, but she refused to let him sidetrack her from her goal. "It is not for me, but for Clarissa and her French lessons."

Five

The colonel paused in the doorway, amused and more than a little impressed by the sight before him. He had not thought it possible to engage his niece's attention in anything outside of herself and her sulks. But now Clarissa bent over a magazine that lay open on her lap, frowning and struggling to get her R's to come from the back of her mouth. She produced instead an inelegant gurgling.

"Think of saying the word as if you had a mouthful of food," Miss Midden suggested. "Or a mouthful of wine. I honestly do believe the language was designed to be spoken only while eating and drinking."

The ladies sat upon a gold brocade couch. Behind them, sunlight streamed in to make a halo of Clarissa's golden curls and added warmth to Miss Midden's sleek brown cap of hair. Magazines lay around them like discarded cannon shells around an artillery battery.

Clarissa wet her lips and read again, "Three narrow *rouleaux*—"

"Yes, that's it," Miss Midden encouraged.

Fashion, Andrew thought, a frown pinching between his eyebrows. The woman was using fashion to teach his niece French . . . what the devil sort of schooling was that?

"—of *gros de Naples* finish the sleeve. The trimming consists of satin *coquings* . . ." Clarissa looked over at

Miss Midden, her forehead wrinkled and her eyes questioning.

"That's a shell-shaped trimming. It comes from the word *coquille* for shell. Of course, you must not mistake that for *coquin,* which is French for rogue."

Clarissa laughed, and the sound echoed in Andrew's ears with a startling unfamiliarity. How long had it been since he'd heard the girl laugh?

Both ladies glanced up suddenly. The laughter fled Clarissa's expression, leaving a militant flash in her eyes. Miss Midden looked vaguely guilty, as if he had found out some terrible secret she would rather keep to herself. And he felt an absolute oaf to have broken into the moment.

"Good afternoon, Colonel," Miss Midden said, recovering her poise. "Will you join us for some tea?"

He hesitated, tempted but uncomfortably aware of Clarissa's resentment. "No, I should not. There's estate business I should attend to."

"I am certain it could wait. And you must think of this as a rescue, for my mouth has begun to hurt from all this French. I had not realized how out of practice I am. Clarissa, would you be so kind as to gather up our discards? Tomorrow we shall have to work harder to find other styles of gown you might like."

"Of course," Clarissa said, folding up the magazine and moving at once to gather the others from the floor.

Andrew lifted an eyebrow at this remarkable obedience, but he knew better than to test his niece's docility too far with a comment. No, he would accept the action and be both grateful and silent.

As Clarissa carried the magazines to a window seat along the far wall, Andrew moved to Miss Midden's side. "*Puis je vous offre mes compliments.*"

Surprise widened her eyes and changed the slate gray to a soft blue. "*Vous parlez très bien le français.* But of course you would have used it much during the campaign against the French. I am a touch rusty, I fear. *Mon français est mauvais.*"

"*Mauvais?* . . . no, not bad. You have a charming accent. And the ability to fasten Clarissa's attention upon something, even if it is a topic that takes up too much of her mind as it is."

Miss Midden's eyes lit with a challenge. "If she were badly dressed, would you credit her with having her mind on higher thoughts?" She did not wait for his answer, but bore on, her voice mild, but her feathers obviously ruffled. "No, you would not. And when she does go to London, she will need to be able to converse with a fashionable modiste. I never did have the vocabulary to say what I liked or disliked, and it did me no end of disservice for the gowns I had made for me."

"Your gowns?" Clarissa asked, returning to them. Awe dawned on Clarissa's face. "But . . . why, you must have had a season, then?"

The smile stiffened on Miss Midden's face, and strain underlined the forced humor in her voice. "Really, Clarissa, I did not leap out full-blown, like an Athena of a governess. Of course I had a season. Years ago, my dear, when I was a girl."

Maeve's face had slowly drained of color, and Andrew could not stop the automatic gesture of touching his hand to her arm. He felt her arm quiver, but she turned and offered a faint smile before moving a step away.

"Shall I ring for tea now?" she asked, but she did not turn around or wait for an answer but busied herself with the bellpull and then moved at once to the door.

He thought he knew what had shaken Miss Midden's poise, and he could have cheerfully boxed his niece's ears for being so tactless. Clarissa's question—voiced with such doubt—had been a sharp reminder of Miss Midden's present station. Whatever had reduced Miss Midden from being a girl with marriage prospects to a single woman with no position or status must carry with it some unpleasant memories. Clarissa's comment must have brought that to Miss Midden's attention.

Clarissa looked ready to pester Miss Midden with even more questions about her past, but Andrew had seen the distress cloud Maeve's blue-gray eyes until they looked like a troubled sea. She did not need more questions, more reminders that she was a woman who must earn her keep. His new title had made him all too uncomfortably aware of the gap between servant and master . . . and Miss Midden occupied the hellish no man's land between.

So when Clarissa opened her mouth to doubtless ask even more embarrassing questions, Andrew interrupted, "Well, Clarissa, do you plan to use your needle to make up some of these French fashions? Do you know, I still have the shirts you made and sent to me in Portugal."

Peach warmed the girl's cheeks, and Andrew realized with a shock that the girl was actually flattered.

"I . . . I have not sewn since . . . in a long while," Clarissa said, her voice thickening.

Have not sewn since Father died . . . that was what she had been about to say. And he had not an idea in the world what to reply, for suddenly his own throat had tightened and his eyes stung. The damn fire must be smoking, he decided, and he went to the grate to stir it, but he found the wood unlit and so he busied himself with lighting it.

When he turned back, he found Miss Midden there and smiling and full of chatter enough to fill the room.

She talked on through tea of inconsequential things. Of the droll fashions in the magazines. Of the need for more current periodicals to tell if hems were going above the ankle or down to sweep the ground. He had always thought talkative women were tiresome, but she had a voice like lemon blossoms, soft but with a hint of tart sharpness in her comments.

She rambled on through tea, pouring for them, offering him Mrs. Henderson's dull cakes and even pushing Clarissa to eat something. And her ramblings inspired him.

"Clarissa, would you like a sewing project? Shall I send you and Miss Midden off to York to buy some fabric?" he asked.

Clarissa's cup clattered into its saucer. "York?"

"I think that's a lovely plan," Miss Midden said, her eyes shining blue.

She honestly had no idea, he thought, how neatly she had just stepped into his trap. And so he looked back at her to meet and hold her stare. "Good. Then you won't mind going with Clarissa, and you will allow her to select material for a new dress for you as well. Even iron rusts and wears out, Miss Midden. I've already had Mrs. Henderson remark on what a pity it is that I do not pay you a decent enough wage for you to properly attire yourself. You cannot allow me to be so badly maligned."

Miss Midden's mouth began to form a stubborn line, but Clarissa intervened. "Uncle is quite right. Every time you take a deep enough breath, I can hear the threads of your seams split apart."

The words—so artlessly spoken—flashed into his mind an image that was anything but innocent. He saw Maeve with her back to him, her brown dress split, offering a tempting sight of creamy skin.

He shook himself, embarrassed by his thoughts and by the reaction his body had offered to them. A lord was not supposed to go around lusting after his niece's governess. She was an employee in his protection, and he was not about to become one of those men who preyed upon women in less fortunate circumstances.

So he ate another of Mrs. Henderson's butter sandwiches and waited for Maeve to capitulate.

Maeve pursed her lips to keep from telling his lordship just what she thought of his tactics to get what he wanted. It might serve his goals very well to have her spend her money on new dresses, for that way she would be lured into staying longer that she might recoup what she had spent. She did not want to waste money that might be needed come that rainy day which had loomed before her for the past nine years. However, she had to begrudgingly admit that one dress would not hasten her to the poorhouse. Nor did it have to make great inroads into her funds.

This did serve her with fair warning. The colonel—his lordship—had beguiled her into forgetting that he was a man accustomed to the use of devious strategy. If she were not careful, she would end up with a longer stay at Rothe House than she intended. And that, she had already decided, simply would not do. She could not afford to stay . . . for she was already starting to like it here too much.

Maeve lay in her bed and stared at the dark ceiling, her eyes now so well adjusted that she could make out the shapes of the plaster, molded into leaves and acorns. Or perhaps grape bunches.

Sleep lay elusively beyond reach, chased away by her too active mind.

She kept thinking of the colonel and his request for her to buy a dress. That notion had stirred in her a forgotten longing for something pretty, for something that might catch his attention. Not something dark and useful. Not something durable. Just a pretty dress. A dress that might warm his eyes when he glanced at her.

But she was being ridiculous.

He was a man with responsibilities. He was a lord, a peer. He was a man who took duty seriously—and his duty to his title and family was to marry a woman of property and family. He had no reason to look at a penniless governess.

She sat up in bed and lit her candle. She had a book to read, but she was not in a mood to read about love and danger and adventure. She needed one of Miss Hannah More's improving books. Or she ought to have picked out one of the colonel's books on drainage.

She could work on her tatting. She had no relatives to send gifts to—or, at least, none who would receive them—but she liked to send out small presents of lace mittens or handkerchiefs at Christmas to past pupils and to some of the other teachers she had worked with in Bath. However, she had no peace in her, and without that she would end up unraveling every bit of lace that she tried to make.

Feeling hot, she threw back her covers and got up to pace.

Exercise. That was what she needed. She knew nothing of the countryside here, however, and she dreaded the thought of getting lost, but the house was large enough to accommodate a midnight stroll. The clock on her mantel chimed, telling her it was indeed half past twelve. A lovely hour for ghosts and restless governesses.

She dragged on a woolen robe, but she left off her slippers. Bare feet would be more silent, and she had a desire to feel the plush of rug under her feet, and to skip lightly over the bare floors. After peering out into the dark hall, she let herself out into the house.

A guilty sense of getting away with something forbidden—and not very like a governess—thrilled her. She was so tired of doing what she always should do. She had tried to discipline this rash side of herself, but it always came out in some fashion. At least this way, she would have it on a leash, like a tame, performing bear.

Silently she padded down the carpeted halls, wandering into passageways made strange by darkness. She smiled and hugged her adventure close to her. She did not need a candle, for her eyes had grown accustomed to the dim light of the sleeping house. Wood floorboards occasionally creaked underfoot, but no one demanded, "Who goes there?"

She wandered up stairs and down hallways, and somehow she ended up standing before the door that led to the burnt-out west wing.

Like a housebreaker, she gave one swift glance behind her, then pushed on the door so that it fell open on well-oiled hinges. She stepped into the roofless room, her mouth open and her eyes pulled upward.

Stars glittered so sharp that she could almost believe what her old nurse had once said about the sky being a velvet cloth in which God had left holes so that man could glimpse bits of heaven. It was heaven here. Under that blanket of sky, her troubles shrank into nothing. Beyond the back of the rooms, the craggy mountains of the Gordale Scar lay like some dark, slumbering beast, their inky blackness blocking the starlight, the moonlight barely glancing off the white limestone cliffs.

She sat down cross-legged, her back against the front wall so that she had a clear view of dark mountains and vivid sky. She felt young again. As young as a child. Her chest tightened with an odd yearning for the home to which she could never return. But she could go back in memory, at least.

Quietly at first, and then made bold by the peace around her, she began to sing a lullaby. It was the only thing she really remembered of the mother who had died when she was only four. It was all she had left now of her family.

* * *

Andrew sat at the desk in his bedroom. His valet—Phillip's man, whom Andrew had inherited along with the title—had been utterly shocked when a desk had been moved into the master bedroom. But eighteen years of hard campaigning had robbed Andrew of the ability to sleep the night through.

Those same years in a campaign tent—or on hard ground—had also left him unable to lie in the huge four-poster bed that had held six generations of Derhursts.

It was too soft. It was too much a lord's bed.

So Andrew had set up his army cot in the room, not far from his campaign desk. Tonight, he had been tired. He had lain down upon the cot and had fallen asleep almost immediately.

The dream had woken him. And he knew better than to try and sleep again after that.

It was always the same dream. He'd started having that nightmare in India, and it had haunted him across Portugal, Spain and to the border of France, and it haunted him still.

It was a damn ridiculous dream. He could have understood dreaming about battle, about horses' death screams and deafening explosions and men howling more like animals. A battle's mayhem would leave anyone in a cold sweat.

He didn't dream that, but he woke, crying, sobbing like a child, filled with shame and self-loathing that he could not control himself or his emotions. It left him unwilling to return to sleep. So now he sat at his desk, looking over estimates for lead roofing, calculating profits from the crops that hopefully would come in this fall, and wishing he was the type of man who could drink himself into a stupor.

Unfortunately—or perhaps fortunately—wine gave

him a pounding headache, and anything much stronger left him clutching at his belly as if it were on fire. So he could not drink himself to sleep, and he was not about to start dosing himself with opium drops the way Dorothy did.

No, he wasn't that far gone.

He stared at his papers a few minutes more, then pushed away from his desk and strode to the window. Perhaps it was simply the restlessness of spring seeping into him. Perhaps it was the habit of night marches on too little sleep. Perhaps it was the feeling of Phillip's presence in this room. Whatever it was, he had to get out.

He started down the hall in his shirtsleeves and stocking feet, his steps aimless. He thought of raiding the kitchens, only Mrs. Henderson would probably blame some hapless servant for his theft from the pantry. He thought of heading to the billiard room, only he was tired of playing against himself. So he wandered until he neared the burnt-out west wing and heard the faint singing.

For an instant, the hair rose on the back of his neck. Childhood stories of ghosts teased the back of his mind. Phillip had terrified him when they were boys with tales of headless knights. However, Phillip was the only ghost in this house, and this voice was distinctly female . . . a throaty siren's call.

His curiosity stirred, Andrew followed the song.

At the door from the main house to the west wing, he paused. The door stood open and the voice floated out, husky, filled with longing, the melody sweetly lifting. He had identified the singer—who else could it be, after all?—but he felt almost as if he should not intrude upon her lone recital. She had obviously come here for solitude. But the urges that had brought him here grew into a stronger desire. He wanted to know what kept her awake

at this ungodly hour, he told himself, even as he knew
that what he really wanted was to see what she looked
like in moonlight. And so he slipped silently into the
room.

Six

She sat on the stone floor in the empty, barren wing. Stars glittered overhead, and he waited for his eyes to grow accustomed to their pale light. She sat with her back against the wall, so that she faced the dark mountains to the east. Her head tilted back so that the newly risen moon spilled silver light onto her face, making shadows of her eyes and turning her skin into white rose petals. Her dark hair disappeared into shadows, and her dressing gown covered most of her form, leaving only her hands, dainty white feet, and the edges of a white nightgown visible.

He frowned as he realized that a faint disappointment was stirring in him. Her voice—so deep and intriguingly feminine—had led him to picture her in something far less mundane than a woolen dressing gown. She ought to be clad in gossamer fairy silk that clung to her form and . . .

He cut off the thought and the irrational disappointment. It was highly unlikely that a governess such as Miss Midden would even own a silk dress, let alone any dress that revealed her other charms. But, by God, did she not at least own a pair of sensible slippers? Had her finances been so restricted that she could not afford them, or was she just not very good at taking care of herself?

Before he could decide the better answer, her lilting melody strangled into a gasp, and he knew that she had somehow sensed his presence. He shifted on his feet, uncomfortable as when he'd been a boy and had been caught stealing strawberry tarts from the kitchen.

The feeling of being intently watched had broken across Maeve like a shaft of light, warming her through. She turned, startled, the song strangled into silence by the tightness in her throat. Governesses were not supposed to serenade the night with sweet song.

It was the colonel who stood silhouetted in the doorway. He was in shirtsleeves and breeches, without even a waistcoat over his open-necked shirt. Moonlight fell over him, outlining his wide shoulders and his form. Of course it had to be him. No one else in the household could generate such a disturbing and concentrated presence. And no one else she knew could stand so silent and solid. It was almost as if he were hewn of the same rock as the walls of this house, cut from those daunting and dark mountains that rose up behind Rothe House.

"I beg your pardon, I did not think I would wake anyone," she said, starting to climb to her feet.

That was a mistake.

In a moment, his long stride brought him to her side and he took her arms, his fingers dark bands over the white sleeves of her nightgown. He pulled her to her feet and then slid his fingers down her arms so that he held her hands between his, rubbing them, warming them and unsettling her.

"You did not wake me. But are you trying to freeze yourself? Your hands are like ice. And why do you not have any slippers on?"

Her face flushed hot. It was her secret that she loved to go barefoot in any weather, to feel solid ground and floor underneath her. But none of that made into a sensible explanation for an answer, and she disliked being caught acting like a child far younger than her charge.

"Nonsense," she said, using her best governess tone. "I've been in cold far worse than this."

"So have I, but not voluntarily." He let out a sigh. "Oh, Miss Midden, what am I to do with you?"

His voice had lost some of its sharpness, and the warmth that scraped low in his tone left her nerveless for a moment. She stared up at his face, seeing only his shadowed eyes and the sharp, pale angles of the hollows of his cheeks.

"Do with me?" she answered, feeling oddly breathless. Then all the old warnings blared. She was a sensible woman far past the age of infatuations and foolishness and longings. She was not a girl to be led astray by her own weakness.

Straightening, she tried to disengage her hands from his, but it was like trying to climb out of the softest feather bed. The more she tugged, the more she seemed to be engulfed in his grip and the less inclined she felt to leave.

Turning away finally allowed her to pull her hands free of his; then she knew that she had better say something or he might think he had upset her.

She put on a bright tone. "I suppose it would look badly to have the governess frozen solid in this ruined wing. I would probably end up haunting Rothe House, and ghosts are such a dreadful nuisance."

He took her hand, his grip light but insistent, and his hold upon her drew her down to sit next to him. She curled her feet tight under her, as if making herself smaller would diminish the awareness of him that almost hummed along her skin.

"Ghosts are more than a nuisance, Miss Midden. And so is a governess who will not have a care for herself. Did you not find your room to your liking? Is that why you wander the house? I can find you another if you prefer. One with lovely, thick, warm carpets."

She could not stop the smile that relaxed her face. She wondered, how was she supposed to stay on her guard against a man who seemed oblivious to the potency of his charm? "My room is lovely. It is nothing to do with that. It is just that I often do not sleep well."

A smile lifted his voice. "I can hardly believe that it is due to a guilty conscience over a scandalous past."

She bit her lower lip and watched him, her eyes straining to see his expression, terrified that somehow he had guessed. But he said nothing more. Slowly she let out the breath she had been holding. He did not know. He could not. He had only been joking.

"No. It could not be from that," she repeated, feeling as hollow as her own voice. "I should go now, my lord."

"Please stay."

She hesitated, caught by the plea in his voice. She sank back upon the hard floor, surprised, and it occurred to her to wonder what it was that had him walking the halls of his own house this late at night.

He looked up, and starlight washed his face in midnight colors of black and silver. A light breeze fluttered the loose sleeves of his shirt. "You pick a charming view for your night revels, and, bare feet or no, I would feel guilty for chasing you away. It is a beautiful sky tonight, but it does make me wonder why beauty always must be so cold and far from reach. Do you have an answer to that question, Miss Midden? Governesses are supposed to have an answer to everything."

In the darkness, she heard more than she ought to. She heard at the heart of his words a bleakness. Of all the curses, loneliness was the worst.

"I wish I did have an answer for everything," she said. "But all I have are opinions. And in this instance, I believe that God meant us to appreciate certain beauty only from a distance. After all, even the most perfect rose, when seen up close, will disclose its thorns . . . and some disgusting bug must always come crawling out of the petals."

His hand tightened over hers, warm and vital, but his voice held humor and not a trace of anything more. "I like that answer. It is both practical and wise. No wonder you make an excellent governess. No, don't try to tug your hand away. I am not going to eat you, and I am not about to allow you to catch a chill sitting here. You are far too valuable to me whole and healthy."

With that, he sat up to tuck her gown more tightly around her feet until not a trace of night air could slip around her ankles. Then he gathered her hands into his, and he sat with them held up to his chest, so that her arm brushed against his.

She stared down at where his darker hands covered her white ones. She was valuable to him. *As a governess, you silly fool.* She must not see more than was here. For all his title, he was a brusque military man, and she must not make him into anything more. He was treating her as if she was his friend, and she must be satisfied with that level of intimacy.

"It seems we are two restless souls, Miss Midden, so we may as well pass the dark hours together. I hate these hours—the ghosting hours. There are ghosts here, you know, but they do not stalk these halls, they wander into my dreams instead. Tell me, my wise Miss Midden, do you know why the good Lord gave us such things as ghosts and dreams to plague our nights?"

"God speaks to us in dreams, if we are to believe the stories of the Bible."

"Then I wish He would speak in good King's English, and not send the same images night after night. Saint Peter should remind the Good Maker that repeat performances become tiresome," he said, the ironic twist back in his words.

She leaned her head against the wall and let her hands lie limp in his grip. "I used to have the same dream over and over. I dreamed about stuffing pillows . . . only I could never get the feathers to stay put, and the more I tried to stuff, the faster the goose down flew out."

He gave a low chuckle. "That would be enough to give you a dislike of any bed, I should think."

"It was not that so much as that I always woke feeling horrible, as if I had failed at some very important task."

She bit her lip and hesitated. It would be improper for a governess to ask her employer personal questions, but considering that he was holding her hands and they were quite improperly alone, she thought the circumstances might allow a question or two.

"What dream or nightmare is it that troubles your sleep?"

"Oh, you don't want to hear about that," he said, his voice clipped and closed.

She pressed her lips tight, then said, "Of course not. You are quite right to give me a set down and correct my misguided interest."

His teeth flashed a smile. "I see the moonlight does nothing to soften your sharp tongue, Miss Midden."

"My lord, you cannot sit there holding my hands, speaking freely to me, and expect me to act as if this were a normal conversation. If you ignore the conventions, you cannot hold me to them."

"I don't think it's the lack of conventions that drew your wrath. I would say it's my presumption in telling you what you ought to do. I wish I'd had you as an officer, Miss Midden. You would have had a crack regiment under your command."

She relaxed again, and he settled his grip even more firmly around her fingers, so that she could feel the calluses on his fingers and the wide span of his palm.

Lowering her voice, she said, "If you tell, they sometimes stop. Mine did."

He shifted, and even with the darkness cloaking his expression, she felt the intensity of his stare. Then he pulled in a breath. She saw his chest rise and fall, and then he turned to stare up at the stars, his profile all uncompromising straightness.

"It always starts with the music," he said, his voice drifting and so low that she had to lean closer to hear.

It was odd to be sitting with him in the darkness like this. They were not lord and governess now—merely two people talking, sharing their warmth, their troubled humanity. The awkwardness of having him hold her hands faded, so that it felt natural to be sitting so close together.

"I don't know where I am, but I'm seated at a piano, and I start to hear the violins and the other strings play. It's dark around me, but I know there is an audience nearby . . . and I settle my fingers on the keyboard and start to play."

"What is it you play? Is it the same song?"

"I don't know. Not really. It's some tune I know . . . only I never remember more than the last dying notes. But as I play, my fingertips begin to numb." He held out one hand and flexed long, elegant fingers. "It's almost as if my hands had been in ice too long. Only it's not like frostbite. I know that sting of cold. This is just . . . just numbness. And the numbness starts to move up from my fingertips to my wrists, and then to my arms. I'm missing notes by then, but the strings keep playing on and on."

His voice dropped to a harsher pitch. She could hear the tension, the smothered feelings. It was not the music, not the dream that bothered him. She knew that from her own dreams. Something else always lay behind them.

"I try to keep up. I force myself. But the numbness spreads to my arms. I want to stand up and run, but I can't pull away. It's as if I'm part of the instrument. It's as if I'm becoming as wooden and hollow . . . and I try to play faster and faster and keep up. Only I can't. I can't do it. And then I start to . . ."

He broke off. She heard the rustle of clothing, and his

breath was smothered as he ran a hand over his face. She could imagine nothing worse for a man such as him than to feel so out-of-control. She could empathize with the near panic and frustration it would cause. And she wondered if it was his loss of the woman he had loved that had caused such a deep fear in him. Or was there something else?

Sitting in the dark, his hands tight over Miss Midden's, Andrew wondered why he had told her all this. He felt an utter fool.

Who else but a fool would cry over a damn piece of music? It was not the friends he had lost that he dreamed of. Not the brother now dead to him. Not the ghastly things he had seen, nor the violence that had left him retching after every battle for the first month he was in service.

No. He woke crying over a rotten piece of music.

He would be damned to hell before he confessed that shameful secret to any living soul.

Instead, he twisted a smile onto his mouth, for even if she could not see it, he felt more in command of himself for being able to put it there. "It's not as good as pillow stuffing, of course, but it manages to get me out of my bed. I have no idea why I should still dream of music when the army's been my life for what seems donkey years."

"Why did you join the army? Was it for a career?"

"Younger Derhurst sons always go into the army, Miss Midden. Or so my father informed me on my eighteenth birthday. I hadn't even given a thought as to what I would do, other than perhaps go to Cambridge or Oxford. But my father laid out the papers for the commission of Ensign that he had purchased as my birthday present. Then he shook my hand, told me to write my mother often, and I left three days later."

Maeve turned full toward him, shocked. She knew—

oh, did she know—that young ladies were totally in the power of their parents to manipulate. She had thought it different for a man. "But how could . . . did you have no say, or wish for a say in your future?"

He lifted one hand, his white shirt fluttering in the dark room. She could picture the look that would be on his face—an expression made hard by so many years of army discipline.

"Regrets are dangerous to indulge, Miss Midden. They leave one far too absorbed in the past, and there's no time for that on the battlefield. I was happy enough with the army, both in India and during the Peninsular War. Then life caught me by surprise again, and my brother died, leaving me his title and his home to look after. I seem to spend most of my life being put into situations I do not expect. First the army. Now my brother's title. I suppose it is no wonder that I dream I cannot stay up with the tempo."

"Yes, but it will come right in time. You are Lord Rothe now, and you will come to feel comfortable in the name as well as in the fact, and then it will be natural for you to want your own family established here."

His voice picked up a hint of amusement. "Now you sound like Dorothy. I think sometimes her greatest fear is that I will supplant her with another Lady Rothe. But I could not do that to her. And I doubt very much that any woman of sense would accept the courtship of a man such as myself—a man with a poor temper, a man with no softness in him. I was a bad bargain as a younger son, and I should not want a woman who desires only a title when there is no heart to be given with it."

She stared at him, wishing she could say something wise now. But she felt far from being very wise. She could not believe that he had nothing to give. He could not be so vital, and she could not feel as she did, if he were as heartless as he believed. She wanted to prove that to him. Instead, she looked down at his hands, and she knew she must leave. What she wanted had nothing to do with this situation. She should not have urged him to confide in her. She should not have allowed this intimacy to blossom.

He was a lord, an honorable man. She was a governess, a woman long ago stripped of her honor. Shame rose in her face as she remembered this. He had almost made her forget.

"I am certain," she said, making her voice as firm as she would for one of the girls in her charge, "that when you take Clarissa to London next year, you will find many ladies very interested in you, Lord Rothe. And while first loves are never forgotten, my lord, they are usually unwise. So do not close yourself to a second, better choice for your lady. And now I think I must go to bed, my lord."

He rose as she did, helping her rise, his touch polite, and she took it as a reminder of just how distant he was from her. How distant he must remain.

"That must be a new record, to have my title hurled at me three times in less than a minute. Have I done something to earn such uncomfortable formality?"

"No, my lord. I mean . . . it is just . . . we should both remember our stations, my lord. After all, I am here for no more than a month or two. And now I bid you good night, my lord." She fled, leaving him alone with the stars and the moonlight.

Andrew stared after her for some time, his thoughts as dark as the world around him. He was a man of thirty-seven, a former colonel in the king's army, a lord now, and he had never felt so perplexed by anything as by Miss Midden. She left him feeling . . . well, he could not even put into words how he felt, for the emotions tumbled around in him with a mixture of amusement, irritation and . . . and something that made him want to peel off that hideous governess attire she hid behind to see what might lay underneath.

Miss Midden. Maeve. Her two identities seemed not at all compatible to him. She was a lady. That was Maeve. Sharp-witted, proud and barefooted. He smiled at the memory of those dainty white feet—quite an appealing image, that. But she was also his niece's companion. A woman of low station and unknown background.

He frowned. She was a puzzle, and he hated puzzles. She was full of surprises, and life had taught him that very little good came from the unexpected. If he had any sense, he would send her back to that damn agency of hers and let her find the position she wanted within a household of girls. But he did not want to send her away. Even less did he want to look at his reasons for keeping her on. He was afraid he would find that they were far less reasonable than he told himself they were.

It made good sense, that was all. Besides, she had presented a challenge to him, and he was not a man who ever backed down from that. No, he would keep her on. He would find out why the devil she sang to herself alone at night. He would unravel the puzzle that was Miss Maeve Midden—and he would convince her to look after Clarissa indefinitely.

He sat down on the stone floor again, and stared up at the stars and left his mind busy with wondering just how he would accomplish his goals.

Seven

Over the next few days, Maeve decided that she had to be more careful of the colonel. No, not the colonel, she had to correct herself—Lord Rothe. A colonel seemed far too accessible a person, while a lord, a peer of the realm, reminded her of the huge gap between their situations. She could not afford to become attached to anyone here, not when she would so shortly be leaving them.

It was not, after all, as if she had to resist his smiles, for he was a man who did not smile often, and she told herself that it was no business of hers to remove the fierce frowns that seemed to be more a matter of habitual expression than any indication of his mood. However, she had something much more difficult to resist—kind treatment. Mrs. Henderson had confessed to Maeve that the colonel—Lord Rothe—had given orders for Maeve to be treated as one of the family. That was a courtesy she had not had in years, and it made her worry all the more that she would grow too accustomed to this place and its people, only to have to leave them.

So at night when she lay in her bed, her mind spinning too fast for sleep, she did not get up to wander back to the ruined wing. She could not stay. She simply could not. If she did stay for a year or so, she would have to go with Clarissa to London when the girl was launched into Society. Sweat dampened her palms at that thought, and the fear and shame swam so thick in her that she thought she would be ill. She could never go back there to the city where her life had wrecked on the rocks of her own folly and reckless yearnings. No, some other companion would have to go with Clarissa to London.

What she had to remember was that the colonel—his lordship—was a man with steel in his eyes, a man who had said he would not make it easy for her to leave. He was not being kind because he liked her, or because he was a kind man. He was simply like any other man who wanted something from her, meaning she could not trust him to think about her needs before his own. And what she needed, she told herself sternly, was a position that offered a lifetime of employment.

She put aside her memory of the night she had sat with him—of how they had talked, of how the rough texture of his hands had felt on hers, of how they had just been two people together. She wrapped up her feelings and folded them away as she had once put aside her wedding dress.

She concentrated instead on waiting for a response from Mr. Jessup in regard to a new position, and on focusing her attention on Clarissa.

That part proved easy. Clarissa absorbed attention. She was not so much spoilt as she was possessed of a vivid imagination, a headstrong will and the usual self-involvement of the young. It was a dangerous combination in a girl. Maeve tried to encourage Clarissa's practical streak—for it was there, buried under the dramatics she used to get the attention she craved—but like any underused skill, it tended to be a last thought, not a first one.

It also proved a continual challenge to find new ways to engage Clarissa's mind.

The girl could stare for hours at a sum, unable to do as simple a thing as divide five hundred by five. But pose the problem as how many bottles of champagne were needed for a ball of five hundred guests, assuming each guest drank a fifth of a bottle, and the division was done instantly. It was not that Clarissa lacked intelligence, Maeve realized; it was that she needed a reason to do the work.

All the talk of balls and gowns and parties had one unfortunate outcome. Clarissa took it into her head that she and Maeve must go to the monthly assembly in York.

When Clarissa made this announcement, Maeve was sitting before a fire with her lace-making in her lap. They had settled in one of the front parlors that afternoon, for the warm spring had given way to drenching rain, and a cozy room seemed the only cure for the disappointment of a canceled picnic.

Maeve glanced out the windows, to the rain-sodden view and the daffodils now flattened against the grass, as she asked in response to Clarissa's suggestion that they go to York, "Are you planning that we should swim there? Or travel by ark, perhaps?"

Clarissa put down the French grammar book she had not been studying. "The rain cannot go on forever. It is certain to clear by this Thursday, and Papa's carriage is a very sound one. It will get us there and back easily."

Maeve picked up her tatting again. "Yes, well, your father's carriage may be very fine, but it is now your uncle's carriage, and we should ask his permission before making any plans. Besides, it is not yet a full year that you have been in mourning, so you cannot yet be thinking of dancing in public."

Clarissa made a snorting sound that ruined her pose of being a young lady on the brink of womanhood, and then she looked very much her sixteen years as she slumped against the sofa where she sat. "It's all his, isn't it? The house. The carriages. Even Mother and I became his when Papa died. It's all so very unfair!"

"Yes, and robins eat worms, as well. Life is not fair to anyone, Clarissa. But you are fortunate that you have an uncle who considers it his responsibility to look after you and who allows you the freedom to continue to live here."

"Well, I shall at least make certain that all my daughters inherit their own houses."

Maeve allowed herself a small smile at this lovely, impossible notion. "In that case, you shall have to marry very rich, or have very few daughters. Houses are not come by cheaply."

"Why did you not marry, Miss Midden?"

Caught off guard, Maeve glanced up and saw Clarissa regarding her. The girl's blue eyes were unusually serious, and a small frown pulled her perfect brows together. Maeve stumbled for an answer that was as truthful as she could keep it. She loathed liars.

"Well, when I was young, I wanted very much to marry, and I . . . I thought I was in love with someone once. In love enough to marry him no matter what anyone said, and that we would live happily ever after."

"What happened?"

"Oh, many things, and not enough things. Suffice it to say, I learned a hard lesson about making decisions with the heart instead of the head. And that it is impossible to love someone you cannot respect."

"Did you stop respecting him? Did he break your heart?"

Maeve shifted, uneasy with where this interrogation might lead. Clarissa was most likely weaving an exaggerated, romantic story in her head that was very far from the sordid truth of the matter.

"I am afraid to confess to a callous heart. It did not so much as crack. But my pride took a severe beating. Now, have you finished attending to your French?"

Clarissa retrieved her grammar book, but then she rose and went to stand beside the window instead of resuming her studies. "What use is it when I never have a chance to practice it? No one ever calls—except to talk estate business with Uncle. Mama will not come down to go and visit anyone, and Uncle terrifies everyone else into staying away."

"Terrifies? Really, Clarissa. Have you ever thought that your neighbors are merely sensitive about your bereavement, and respecting the fact that you are not yet ready to start coming out of mourning? After all, Lord Rothe is no ogre."

"He might as well be. He will not make the least effort to be social. He says it is all up to Mama. And she . . . well, it was different when Papa was here. Everyone loved him."

Maeve lowered her tatting again and studied the girl's still profile. A pout pulled down Clarissa's full lips, but the pain that had darkened her eyes could not be mistaken.

"You miss him a great deal, don't you?" Maeve asked softly.

Clarissa wiped at the wetness that gathered near the corner of her eye. "It is no matter. As Uncle says, tears will not bring him back, and Mama cries enough for the both of us." She turned to Maeve and put on a bright smile. "Oh, do let us go to the assembly, Miss Midden. I am so tired of never getting to do anything anymore. And Uncle Andrew did say we might go shopping, so we could just stay on a night for the assembly. Can't we . . . please?"

Maeve took up her tatting so that she would not have to look at the pleading in those huge blue eyes. That look must melt anyone's heart.

"An assembly is quite a different matter than a day at the shops. Perhaps we should wait until your mother feels up to taking you."

"But that will be forever. Mama will never be better."

Maeve looked up, alarmed at the thought that Clarissa believed Lady Rothe was dying. "You must not think that, Clarissa. You mother will get better."

Clarissa threw herself down on the sofa again. "How can she, when there is nothing wrong with her? I've heard the doctors talking to Uncle, and they can't find anything wrong. It is just that she doesn't want to do anything with Papa gone, and she doesn't care . . . well, I suppose I am not much of a consolation to her."

Maeve's heart twisted at the wistful longing in Clarissa's voice. She got up and crossed the room to take Clarissa's hand. It lay cold and limp in hers. "You must not take your mother's problems on your shoulders."

"But—"

"We all make our own choices in life, and if your mother chooses to turn her back to the world, that choice has nothing to do with you or how she feels about you. It is her problem, not yours. Do you understand that?"

Clarissa bit down on her lower lip and gave a small nod, her eyes still luminous with unshed tears.

"As to York and the assembly . . ." Maeve hesitated, uncertain about the wisdom of what she was about to say, and aware she was probably acting rashly. But she also knew that if Clarissa was not given some outlet for her energy and her fantasies, they would build up, allowing the first unscrupulous fellow who came along to take advantage of them. She swore to herself that would not happen here.

"As to such outings." Maeve began again, her voice firm, "I shall ask your mother about it this afternoon, and if she thinks it a good idea, I shall speak to Lord Rothe."

Clarissa wrapped her arms around Maeve in a startling, fierce hug. "Oh, I'm so glad you came to us, Miss Midden. And we shall buy new dresses in York, and have tea and cakes and actually see people!"

"I cannot promise anything. But you had better polish your French, miss, if you are to try it out in public."

"Oh, I will, I will, I will," Clarissa said, already up on her feet. "Should I wear my blue dress, do you think? No, it should be white, should it not, since I am not really out, and Mrs. Henderson must help me find a blue ribbon to trim it with . . . and we must find you something to wear. Perhaps I could alter one of Mama's old dresses for you? You would not mind, for they are very pretty, and Mama couldn't fit into any of her older dresses. And I promise I'll speak only French as I sew, Miss Midden."

Clarissa danced out the room before Maeve could get another word out. She watched the girl go, her own enthusiasm and resolution slipping away with Clarissa. Now how was she to convince everyone else in this house that it was a good idea to allow Clarissa to go to the York assembly?

The subject came up easily that afternoon when Maeve took up tea for Dorothy, Lady Rothe, but Maeve had not expected her ladyship's reaction.

"Go to a public ball. My little girl?" Lady Rothe said, putting her teacup down with a nervous clatter. "I don't . . . well, you shall have to ask her uncle. Now, are there any more of those little iced cakes on the tea tray?"

With that, Lady Rothe dismissed the subject and resisted every effort Maeve gave to the notion that it should be Lady Rothe who actually approached his lordship on the matter. Her ladyship soon pleaded a headache, and Maeve noticed that Lady Rothe did indeed look pale and unhappy. Obviously, her ladyship did not believe that such an outing would be a comfortable topic to discuss.

So it was all left to Maeve.

At dinner that evening, she saw both the inquiring look that Clarissa gave her as well as the fatigued slump to Lord Rothe's shoulders. He had been in his study all day, going over plans with his architect, and if it had been in

Maeve's power, she would have put dinner back an hour and ordered him to rest before the meal.

However, it was not her place to tend to him, so she simply set about to wait for a suitable opportunity to bring up the subject of York.

Clarissa did not help matters by dropping heavy hints about how nice it would be when the rain broke and they could go out and about again.

Lord Rothe glanced at his niece. "And where is it, pray, that you are wishing so hard to go? Is there some particular scheme you have afoot, miss?"

"Yes," Clarissa said.

"No," Maeve contradicted at the very same time. She frowned fiercely, and Clarissa at least had the good conscience to blush and drop her gaze.

"I see," Lord Rothe said, glancing from Maeve to Clarissa, and looking very much more like a colonel surveying his subordinates rather than a lord eating his dinner. "Perhaps, Miss Midden, you would be so kind as to explain these contradictory answers after the meal."

"Did I tell you that I had a letter from Sybil Tremont today, Uncle?" Clarissa said, changing the topic and studiously cutting the pigeon on her plate.

"Who, pray, is Sybil Tremont?"

"She is only Squire Tremont's eldest girl, as you would know if you ever took the trouble to meet our neighbors, and she is only a year older than me, and already in London this season. She has already been to any number of balls and assemblies."

Maeve's insides knotted with worry for the scene that threatened. Clarissa had that look in her eyes—the one that mirrored her uncle's in determination—and she was going to spoil everything if she simply romped into announcing the idea of going to an assembly. The colonel was in no mood to give a kind answer, and Clarissa seemed unable to see that.

"Clarissa," Maeve interrupted, putting every effort at firm censorship into her tone, "I doubt if your uncle is much concerned with the literary efforts of your friend."

Clarissa's mouth pulled into a pout, and anger sparked in her eyes. Thankfully, before she could say anything, the dining room door opened and a footman hurried into the room. In the hall outside Maeve spotted a man in rough clothes, talking to Mrs. Henderson, who anxiously clasped her hands together. Clarissa shot a look of inquiry at Maeve, who only shook her head and sent a silent plea for Clarissa to stay mute.

The footman bent and muttered something to Lord Rothe. His lordship's frown darkened until Maeve dared not ask what was the matter.

Lord Rothe rose suddenly, throwing his napkin down and striding to the door, his step brisk and his back military straight. "Finish your meal," he ordered, snapping out the command, his thoughts obviously very far from the fact that he was in civilized company.

Then he was out the door, the footman on his heels. The door rattled in its hinges as he shut it behind him.

"Well, what do you think that was all about?" Clarissa asked.

Maeve drew in a breath. "I am not sure if it was a heaven sent interruption or a very bad omen. Clarissa, I have not spoken to your uncle about any assembly, yet, and I beg you to allow me to broach that topic in my own time. If you honestly wish to go, then you must wait for the right moment to present itself. Timing is an art every lady must learn."

Clarissa lowered her head, repentant for an instant, but then she looked up, her eyes bright with curiosity. "Something awful has happened, hasn't it? Why else would he have looked so grim? Do you think someone from his army past has come to seek revenge on him, and that there will be a duel perhaps, or a terrible fight on a cliff with lightning flashing overhead?"

"I think we should do as we were bade and finish our meal," Maeve said, her own imagination no less active than Clarissa's, but a good deal more prosaic in the troubles it invented. She wondered if she would have the chance tonight to ask Mrs. Henderson just what had happened.

The rest of the evening passed quietly, with Clarissa restless and without Lord Rothe's return. Mrs. Henderson brought the tea to the drawing room at nine. She had no news to relay of what had taken Lord Rothe out of the house, other than that the rough-clothed man he had left with was Seth Wilton, a tenant farmer, who had arrived with word of storm damage to one of the pastures.

This lack of drama disappointed Clarissa, and when Maeve took the girl up to spend an hour with Lady Rothe, instead of reading, mother and daughter spent the time inventing harrowing—and outlandish—stories as to what might have pulled his lordship away from his dinner.

Maeve found it a silly exercise that did nothing to soothe her own certainty that something was indeed wrong. She did not care for the images of death, disaster and tragedy that left the other women breathless and intrigued.

When the clock struck half past ten, Maeve excused herself for bed.

Only she could not sleep.

She lit her candle and read from *Ivanhoe*—for the wounded Ivanhoe was still being cared for by the brave Rebecca. That was drama she could enjoy. When her candle flame guttered out, she added coal to the banked fire and went to sit beside her window.

Outside, the world lay dark and colorless. Clouds hid most of the sky, but the wind had come up and allowed fitful glimmers of light from the new moon. Pale light would dance for a moment on the wet grass and leaves and then the world would turned dark again.

His lordship had still not returned, at least not by the front door, which lay in view from this side of the house. Maeve watched every shadow, her own imagination more active than Clarissa's now, her hands clenched tight on the cloth of her dressing gown. It was not a night to be out so late, and the later it grew, the more Maeve worried. Only bad news would keep him from home for so long.

When the hall clock struck one, Maeve could bear her own restless suspense no longer. She remembered to put on her slippers, and then she left her room. She had to see if he had come home by another entrance.

Andrew came into the hall exhausted and wet. The rain had stopped hours ago, but not before giving him a drenching as he had ridden out. And to do what? To sit and watch as a good portion of his south fields slipped into the river. He had been useless. Worse than that, he had been helpless.

One man had lost his life trying to save a stupid, ill-fated sheep from the river that had overrun its banks and cut deep into the pastures. God knows how many others would catch an illness from this night's soaking. And what had he been able to do about it?

Damn all.

He had watched, like the others, as the river cut out the ground and the man simply vanished. And he'd been able to do nothing.

After that, he had told the rest of the men to forget the damn sheep, that the estate would cover the losses. He would see to it that the widow of the drowned man was cared for, but that would not bring her man back to her. Such a senseless incident in a senseless world.

He shivered. The cold had gone deeper than through

his garments. It seemed to have penetrated to his soul. What the hell did he know about managing an estate? Should he have foreseen the river's flood and had the sheep moved to higher ground? Was this an accident he might have prevented if he had been paying more heed to the land and its people, rather than to his plans and damnable estate accounts? Why had he never paid attention when he and Phillip had both been growing up in this house?

His muddy boots left a path across the floor as he went to his study and found the brandy. The liquid slid down his throat hot as a firebrand and seared into his stomach, but did nothing to warm him. He put down the glass and started up the stairs, his steps dragging, his shoulders aching. Then he stopped.

She sat on the top step of the staircase, as if she were waiting for him. She looked ridiculously anxious and young with her hair in a braid that fell over her shoulder and a silly white nightcap upon her head.

He gave her a tired smile. "Miss Midden, I hope you have slippers on tonight, for it is too cold a night for bare feet."

"Your clothes are wet," she said, rising. "I am not the one who will catch a chill tonight."

"I'm a lord now. I ring for servants and they jump to obey my commands," he said, thinking bitterly of how little he had been able to command his world tonight.

She glanced at him from the corners of her eyes. "You won't wake them, will you? Mrs. Henderson has already told me that you sleep upon an army cot. And do not think to blame her for gossiping. It shocks her to her soul that you are a lord and will not use a bed like a proper Christian."

He smiled and thanked heavens that his brisk governess was here to greet him and turn his world back

to the ordinary. "I had not realized I was such an improper lord."

"You are. You are also an obstinate man, but in this
case, I will ask you to yield to me. You are too tired to
take care of yourself, and someone must."

She took him by the hand and led him down the hall.
He let her, for he was far too tired to argue or resist. He
felt reduced to being a boy again, with no weight of responsibility on him, and it was a blessed relief to have
her small, warm hand close over his. He allowed his mind
to stop turning and simply followed her command. She
smelled of lavender and looked deliciously like a girl, not
a governess, so slim and barely reaching up to his shoulder with the top of her head, and he liked the way the
end of her braid dangled, tempting him to pull it.

He hesitated only when opened the door to her own
bedroom.

She turned to him, her expression cross, and yet looking ridiculously prim with that white cap upon her head.

"It is the only room with a fire that I know of," she
said, "Unless you gave orders to have someone wait up
for you?"

He actually felt a tingle of embarrassment on his
cheeks. She was quite right. He had left orders for the
exact opposite, but he still felt awkward. "I told them not
to wait up," he admitted.

"I thought as much. So you will please to come into
my room, my lord. Actually, it is your room in your house,
so you have every right to be here. And I shall promise
not to do anything that might compromise you."

"Me? What of your own reputation?"

"I haven't had one of those to worry about in years,
thank heavens. A governess only needs good references,
which you cannot very well give to me if you take a chill
and die."

She tugged him into her room, shutting the door behind

them and bullying him into a wing-backed chair near the
dying fire. He relaxed into the chair, wondering when it
was that he had last sat down and if he would be able to
get up again, and if he had the strength to lift his legs up
to put them on the footstool beside the chair.

She poked fresh flames from the embers and added
more coal. Then she turned and surveyed him, her hands
on her hips, which molded her shapeless dressing gown
to her slim waist. "We must get those boots off you . . .
and your jacket looks ruined by the wet."

"Leave them, Maeve. Sit with me. The fire will dry
me well enough, and after having all the rains of Spain
drench me, I'm not like to take my death from this wet-
ting—not that my passing would offer much bother to
anyone."

She stepped forward and stood over him, her eyes spar-
kling with anger, her hands now fists at her side. "Someone should box your ears—lord or no—for speaking in
such a way. No bother, is it? What do you think Clarissa
will do if she loses her uncle as well as her father? And
Lady Rothe? Do you think she has no feelings?"

"They will adore the opportunity to dress dramatically
in black again, which I was only just able to make them
put away. And I have a cousin somewhere who will make
a much better Lord Rothe than I ever shall."

"But will he love them as you do? Oh, I know you
complain of them, but if you really did not care, you
would pack them off to some other part of the country—
and you easily could. You must have a dozen houses to
your title. Or you could live in London and ignore them
utterly. If you did not care, you would not be here, trying
to forge something of a family."

He shifted in his chair, uncomfortable with her as-
sessment of him and his motives. Of course he cared.
But love? No, that was not a sentiment he had the time
or the inclination to indulge. He was a man who did

his duty and honored his responsibilities. That was why he was here.

"Miss Midden, you have as vivid an imagination as Clarissa to read all that into my actions."

She turned to stir up the fire with the poker again. "Very well, you don't care. And neither do I."

His temper snapped and new energy surged into him, making him sit up. "It is not an issue of caring, it is about doing what is expected of me. My brother left me his family to look after, Lord help us all. I have a duty to them, and while Dorothy is a grown woman and beyond anyone's help, I am damn well not going to allow Clarissa to run wild, simply because it would be easier for all concerned not to cross her will."

Maeve replaced the poker and turned back to him. A prim, satisfied smile curved up the corner of her mouth, and Andrew knew when he had been gulled into a trap.

"You, Miss Midden, have goaded me on purpose, have you not?"

"Well, it was obvious to anyone that you were in a mood to feel sorry for yourself. Pity should be reserved for those who can honestly do nothing about their situation, and that is not you, though you may occasionally feel that way."

"No, it's not me. I'm a lord now . . . I can do anything," he said, staring into the fire, his voice thick with sarcasm and self-loathing.

Maeve's teeth ground. If she'd had a vase of flowers close to hand she would have emptied its contents over his head. "Really, sir, you sound no better than Clarissa in one of her sulky moods. So you think you ought to be able to do anything? Even adjust the laws of God and nature to suit you?"

He looked up at her, his face haggard. "What God is it that allows a man to die for no better reason than a damned sheep?"

"You think perhaps there are good reasons to die? For honor, perhaps? Or one's country? The world is what the world is, my lord. We live and we die, and the reasons for either do not really matter. Those are events far beyond anyone's control. It is only what lies between those two events that we can affect, and give some reason to our lives by our works and choices. What if God were to step in and answer every single prayer—including yours that this man did not have to die? What about those armies, with both sides praying to God for victory? And there are a few people I have prayed to be struck dead, and I am very glad that God had the wisdom not to listen to me then. And . . . and I have said too much, haven't I?"

He had leaned back in his chair, a tired amusement lightening his eyes. The lines had relaxed in his face and she realized again what a handsome man he was when he looked like this.

Maeve folded her hands in front of her, locking her fingers so tight that they tingled. She had stepped far beyond the bounds of how a governess should speak to her employer, but she would not take back a single word. He was too good a man to spend his life in useless regrets.

She lifted her chin as he studied her, and her cheeks burned a little under his scrutiny, but she did not look away. She was prepared to hear any rebuke he chose to give her.

"You are right, Miss Midden, as always. Perhaps it is just that I thought when I left the battlefields of Spain behind, I also left the specter of death. I did not expect to meet with it again so soon."

She was not prepared for him to admit this, and she looked away then, startled by the tears that suddenly tingled in her nose and stung her eyes. He sounded so weary.

"What is it? I've said something wrong, haven't I? Should I have dressed you down? I can never seem to remember when I should act the lord. I misspent my youth with my head full of music, with no eyes to see anything but notes and no ears to hear anything but the tunes in my head. I'm well served now by having to do all the things which I ignored because I always thought they would fall to Phillip, so you must forgive my stumbling ways."

He sat up and reached for her hand. She tried to wave him away, but he caught her arm and pulled her down so that she sat on the footstool before him.

She stared at his hands, which lay over hers, his skin so much darker than hers, his grip so much stronger.

"I beg your pardon, my lord," she said, keeping her voice formal and controlled. "I had no right to take you to task as I did. I should not have waited up for you, but I was worried when you left the table as you did, and I never did have the chance to talk to you about Clarissa."

"Ah, Clarissa. Of course, you waited up to talk to me about Clarissa."

She glanced up, puzzled by the disappointed tone in his voice, but his expression showed nothing more than fatigue and his usual frown.

"My lord, I know you care for her. I wish you could see that she really is a good girl. She is just a touch bored. She has no sister or brother to keep her company. She needs to get out and about, and meet young people her own age."

"You sound as if you are trying to argue yourself out of a position. The longer she stays in the schoolroom, the longer you could remain here with us, you know."

His argument was as persuasive as his voice, and Maeve allowed herself one moment of longing that this could be true. However, she knew the more likely outcome, and it would not be a happy, long-term position with Clarissa forever content in her schoolroom.

Maeve drew her hands back and sat on the footstool,

her back as straight as an iron poker. "I must argue in Clarissa's interests as well as my own. I very much fear that if you delay her entrance into society too long, you will create the potential for a scandal that might well end my career. Clarissa is too lively to stay content with books alone. She needs amusements to keep her out of mischief. Personally, I believe that original sin would not have occurred had Eve been kept busy naming some of the animals with Adam. Clarissa needs that same approach."

"Miss Midden, your interpretation of the Bible is entertaining, but it does not sway me. Clarissa must demonstrate that she is capable of behaving herself in company before I allow her to go out and possibly land herself in that scandal which so worries you."

"And how can she learn to behave in company when she is never in company? That is a man's logic. You must think, instead, as a father, for you are one to her now. You must think with your heart just a little, and give her some opportunities to show you that she can behave. And a small, local assembly is just the place for that."

"Think with my heart?" he asked dryly. "I do not even think I have such an organ any longer. It must have atrophied from lack of use by now."

She frowned at him. Perhaps this was not the time to tease him. He was so very tired. But sitting there, his clothes still damp and clinging to him, his face softened a little by the late hour, he did not look intimidating. What had she—or he, for that matter—to lose if she pressed him now?

She took a breath and dove in, attacking straight to the fear that had driven her to speak in the first place.

"Well, if you cannot think like a father, then put yourself in the shoes of a man who is looking for opportunity. If you were a fortune hunter, would you try for a girl who has been out in society and who knows the difference between flattery and sincere admiration, or would you go after a girl who is too green to know how to protect herself?"

His mouth tightened. She waited, letting him dwell on that thought. She could see that he did not like the images she had conjured, but someone had to warn him of the dangers that Clarissa faced. The girl was far too pretty— and had far too large a dowry—to be anything but a temptation to the wrong type of man.

"You don't give me much choice in the matter," he said finally, his voice grim.

Her heart sank. He had made up his mind. She could hear that in the finality of his tone. He was not going to listen to her arguments.

Then he smiled at her. A sudden warmth rushed up her arms and fled to her head, making her as giddy as if she had been standing in the summer sun.

"If I learned anything from Wellington, it is how to retreat in good order when a battle is lost."

He rose, and she stood as well, but she still had to look up at him. He was close enough that she could smell the damp rain on his clothes, and the smoke of the fire wove around them like a mist. She felt very small . . . or was it that he just seemed so overwhelmingly strong?

She looked down, her heart beating fast, afraid that her feelings were too apparent on her face, and that he might mistake her gratitude for something else.

He took her chin, making her look up again. "There is no need to look so smug, Miss Midden. I promise you only a lively trip to York. No assembly. Not yet, at least. And there is one condition I make of you. You must put away this notion of leaving us until after this trip is planned and executed. Will you promise me that?"

She stared up into the black depth of his eyes. A small voice at the back of her mind kept repeating that she must be the greatest fool on earth, but she didn't care. She nodded agreement, her lips parting to say, "I'll stay."

She heard the words come out as if someone else had said them. She was mad to say any such thing.

The frown returned to his face, pulling his black eyebrows together. "You should have a better care for what you promise me, you know. I'm a man who does not relent on vows given." He touched the tip of one finger to her cheek with the barest of caresses, as if he could not stop himself from making the gesture. Then he quickly turned, his hands folded behind his back as he strode from her room.

Maeve sank back onto the footstool, her mind spinning, and the good sense that had been clamoring at the back of her mind now in control again.

What had she just done? Had she really promised to stay for some unspecified amount of time? She had extracted from him no similar promise that the trip to York would occur shortly. She had, in fact, just tossed her future into his hands.

She had no idea if, as the sensible part of herself urged, she ought to be worried, or if she ought to give into the guilty pleasure that still tingled on her skin. Oh, she was in very dangerous waters, and she seemed to be willfully swimming deeper and deeper without a care where her reckless heart would lead.

Eight

Over the next few weeks, the colonel honestly did not try to find excuses to postpone the trip to York. Fate simply conspired to allow him ample reasons to put off the expedition, meaning that it was less likely that Miss Midden would leave them, which was exactly what he wanted. Habit, after all, he reasoned, was a powerful force to overcome, and Miss Midden had settled nicely into the habits of Rothe House.

Thankfully, Clarissa did not seem to mind the delays. She seemed so much caught up in the anticipation of the event that he wondered why he had not thought about using this particular carrot before to achieve such a sunny mood from the girl. He felt only the slightest guilt that he was using it on her now, and he put aside that feeling as easily as he had put aside all others for the past eighteen years.

Of course, they'd had to wait for the roads to dry; then it was Miss Midden who had come down with a cold; and then lambing season started. The excuses seemed quite understandable and not at all manufactured, but he knew underneath all the rationalization that it was a bad general who delayed too long an unwelcome campaign. The trick was, how long a delay could he afford without jeopardizing Miss Midden's goodwill?

Miss Midden, maddeningly, seemed to accept her enforced stay with a calm demeanor that gave away nothing of her true feelings. However, he noted that she still checked the post every morning for news of a new position, and he had glanced up more than once after dinner to find her watching him. She would inevitably lower her stare, the faintest stain of a blush warming her cheeks, which left him wondering if she had been staring at him with provoked irritation, or with some other emotion.

It bothered him that he could not guess her thoughts, and like a thorn under his skin, this festered into an ungentlemanly inclination to see if he could delay this trip long enough to goad her into losing that placid exterior. He still had the feeling that he had not yet seen the true Maeve. And he wondered every night before he closed his eyes why she had chosen a life that required her to hide her trim figure behind hideous dresses and her quick mind behind a governess's deferential manners.

Which was why, one morning, when he heard someone playing the pianoforte in the drawing room, he allowed himself to be lured in that direction.

The door stood open, so he pushed it wide on well-oiled hinges, hoping that he would surprise Miss Midden there. Instead, time rushed backward twenty years at the sight before him, and for an instant all the pain of youth, the exquisite longing, the awkward uncertainty, the thrill and the desperation, rose in him as if they had never been banished.

The room was large, with wide casement windows that stretched from floor to ceiling along the east wall. Morning sunlight streamed in from those windows, softened by gauze curtains, spilling across the blond wooden floor like shafts from heaven. The walls were white with gilt trim, and life-size portraits of past Derhursts gave splashes of dark color, but it was the girl seated at the pianoforte which riveted his attention.

She sat facing away from him, so that he could see only her blond curls and slim figure. *Dorothy,* he thought for an instant, the name echoing in his head and his chest as clearly as the notes from the pianoforte rushed to his ears. Then the girl struck a wrong note, and time slipped back to its normal flow.

Of course it was not Dorothy. It was Clarissa. He let out the breath he had held so long that his chest ached with it, and then he realized with a sliver of anger digging into him that the music had played its trick on him. Damnation, he knew that tune. The question was, where had Clarissa learned it?

He strode into the room, his boots echoing on the wood floor. Clarissa stopped playing and glanced over her shoulder. He must have been scowling, for the girl scrambled to her feet, half stepping on her hem and nearly tearing it, her eyes wide and looking for all the world as if she were afraid that he might beat her. If he'd had any sense, he should have done just that when she had first tried her tempers on him, but he couldn't then and he could not now, so he merely scowled at her and demanded, "Where the devil did you learn that song?"

She nervously ran her thumb along a crack in the side of the pianoforte. The instrument had been old in his youth, and no one had ever much cared for it, other than himself.

"I . . . Papa taught it to me," she said, her tone uncertain.

"Your father couldn't carry a tune to save his . . ." Andrew broke off, realizing that he was about to make an even worse hash of it with his analogy.

However, Clarissa's temper had been roused. Her eyes flashed and her chin came up as she said in defense of her father, "He was not particularly musical, but he could hum a tune quite credibly, and I could pick it out and put it together."

"Well, you've gotten this one all wrong."

"I have not! I play it exactly as Papa taught me. And how would you know if it was wrong?"

"I ought to know. I wrote it."

Her mouth fell open in surprise; then curiosity overcame temper. "Really? I mean, Mama said you had played, but I thought . . . well, I'd heard you burnt all your music."

He stepped closer to the ancient pianoforte and touched one finger to an ivory key. He did not press hard enough to sound the note. "I did. That particular piece I wrote for . . . I wrote it for your father's twenty-fifth birthday. He must have recalled it from memory."

Shyly smiling, she stepped closer. "Would you play it for me? As you played it for him? Please?"

For an instant, the temptation to break his vow almost overwhelmed him. Clarissa had never before asked anything from him, and his fingers itched to be on the keys, to flow over them, to have the music quicken at his touch again.

Sanity came back with a rush. He backed away from the instrument. His father might be long dead, but Andrew had given his word. While he might not have music in his life, he still had honor.

"I can't," he said, staring at the instrument, a shameful longing for the feel of it still eating at him.

Clarissa stiffened and glared at him.

He could not? More like he would not. Clarissa nearly turned on her heel and stormed out. She had made such a simple request—one she had thought would bring her a touch closer to the memory of her father—his own brother. Yet he had not the manners to even phrase his refusal in anything but curt, ungracious words.

Before she could turn away, however, the look in his eyes caught at her and made her hesitate.

It was a look that reminded her of her father. Her throat tightened with tears, but she could not say if they were for her uncle, her father, or herself. She had not often seen that look in her father's eyes, but it had appeared a few troubled times. It came with a strained tightness, and a heart-tugging emptiness, as if nothing would ever be right again. She had always been able to charm her father out of such a mood, but she had no idea what to do with her uncle. She only knew that her father would have expected her to do something. The dreadful man was her father's brother, after all. He was her family.

She cast a glance around, wondering what to do, then hit upon an idea. Seating herself at the pianoforte, she arranged her skirts with a flourish.

"Very well, if you cannot, then you must tell me what I am doing wrong. Is it the tempo?" She began to play, deliberate and dragging, determined to at least give him a small punishment for his curt refusal. "Or perhaps there should be an arpeggio here?"

She ran her fingers across a trill of notes, smiling at the effect and starting to enjoy herself.

"Good God, no," Andrew blurted out, the words dragged out of him by the utterly appalling things this child was doing to what had once been a lovely, simple sonata.

"Well, if you will not show me or tell me how it is to be played, then I must make up my own bits to go with it."

Andrew glared at her, but she kept her eyes focused on her fingers and he found himself helpless to do anything. The child was a minx, a devil in skirts, a danger to the world—and she damn well knew it.

He folded his hands behind his back, started to stride out, and then winced as Clarissa added a minor chord. He stopped, the pulse pounding in his jaw; then he turned and strode back to her.

"The tempo is two-four time, miss . . . like this." He began to tap on the pianoforte's open lid. "One-two. One-

two. Do not drag. Now just play the melody you learned
from your father."

He closed his eyes and listened as she carefully picked
out the notes. "Yes, good. No, it's D to E, then back to
C."

She threw up her hands suddenly. "Oh, this is no good.
If you will not show me, how can I learn? Can you not
at least hum it for me? I was very good with Papa in
picking up what he could hum, but he always said that
you had the voice in the family, not him."

Andrew stood there, his hand stilled upon the cracked
varnish of the ancient pianoforte. His niece's eyes had
stormed over to flashing sapphire, and she waited with
her arms folded and her mouth pulled into a mutinous
pout.

His promise had included all instruments, but did that
include the voice? His throat tightened automatically as
the conflict of duty and his own desires clashed, but
Clarissa raised her eyebrows in such an exact copy of
one of Phillip's challenging stares that he damned himself
as a fool. Then he cleared his throat and started to sing
the melody.

Maeve heard the low baritone voice coming from the
drawing room and entered, as a good companion should,
prepared to find Clarissa with some previously unknown
neighborhood beau in her thrall and ready to provide a
proper chaperoning. She stopped in the doorway, taken
aback by the sight of the colonel, Lord Rothe, singing.

His voice carried clearly, only the faintest huskiness
hinting at a lack of practice.

Maeve watched, utterly astonished, as Clarissa bent
over the keyboard and began to accompany him, picking
out the notes to match the tune he set.

The smile that rose up in Maeve reached from her toes

to her lips. *They have found something in common after all*, she thought, a tingle of pleasure racing over her face. She knew she should leave them, but she could not help indulging herself with watching the enjoyment blossom on Clarissa's smile, with seeing the colonel's dark eyes begin to gleam.

The colonel was not much of a savage beast, but Maeve had always thought music held more than the power to soothe. It held the power to heal.

As she thought this, the colonel looked up, his gaze drawn to her by some invisible thread. The song died on his lips and the smile died in his eyes. A dusky color stained his tan cheeks, turning them bronze.

Good Lord, he's actually blushing, she thought, then realized he would not be put in the best of moods by this interruption. She had learned that he was not a man who cared to be caught off his guard.

Clarissa looked up at her uncle, then followed his stare to the doorway, and the music died in the room.

"Pardon me," Maeve said. "I did not mean to intrude. I . . ."

She could not think of an excuse she could give. To say she had suspected that Clarissa was entertaining gentlemen seemed hardly the thing to say when she was trying to impress upon Lord Rothe how proper his niece could be in company.

The colonel folded his hands behind his back. "It's not an intrusion, Miss Midden. I had not meant to stay. Do play the tune as you like, Clarissa."

He started to stride out, but Clarissa leapt up and caught at his arm. "Oh, please do not go. There is a duet I have longed to practice, only I cannot, for Miss Midden is but one voice and I cannot play and sing at the same time no matter how hard I try. Please, please, Uncle, will you not stay for one song . . . you have such a wonderfully strong voice."

Maeve had no idea what was in Clarissa's mind, but she knew some plot was afoot. Clarissa played the pianoforte when she was bored with every other occupation. She did not long to practice at anything. The girl was also staring at her uncle with such a wickedly melting gaze that Maeve wondered how any man could resist.

The colonel was made of sufficiently stern stuff that he at least hesitated.

"Please," Clarissa added, her smile turning wistful, her dark lashes dropping slightly over her wide blue eyes.

The colonel acquired a slightly hunted look and shifted on his feet as if his boots had suddenly shrunk. Maeve decided at once that Clarissa had opened a breach in the colonel's defenses, and reinforcements were now needed to see if they could tear down those stony walls he had put around himself.

Maeve came forward, adding her coaxing to Clarissa's. "A duet sounds lovely. My lord, I presume you have not forgotten how to read music?"

As she expected, her comment sparked a dark eyebrow to rise with scorn. He hesitated a moment longer, seeming to weigh the situation, then gave in with better grace than Maeve had expected.

"Of course I can still read music, Miss Midden. I am not certain I will offer much harmony here, however."

"Well, then we shall both sing melody and try not to fall too far out of step, shall we?" Maeve said, feeling every bit as devilish as Clarissa had been to dragoon him into this.

"There's only the one sheet of music, so you shall have to share," Clarissa said, pulling the sheet from the piano bench before she seated herself again. She struck up the tune's introduction.

Maeve glanced up at the colonel. His expression gave away nothing as he held out the music for her to read alongside him, so she turned her attention to the music and started to sing.

His deep voice complemented her throaty contralto. The music did not tax her limited powers, and she found that his voice provided more strength to hers. He departed from the melody and began to sing counterpoint to her, and she began to lose herself in the pure pleasure of the moment.

She glanced up at him, lured by the easiness between them as their voices wove together, the notes soaring, his deeper tone sounding the harmony to the melody she set. It was only for an instant that their eyes met. Awareness of him—of his muscular arm against hers, his presence towering next to her, his deep voice vibrating in her chest—swept over her and through her.

The last note stilled, and Maeve dared not look up again. She did not trust herself, and she dared not trust him. She was a sensible woman, and she was going to act like it—but she did not feel that way at all.

The colonel cleared his throat and said, his voice all military brusqueness, "Clarissa, you need a new instrument to play. That one never could keep a tune. I'll buy you one in York."

He started to stride out, but Clarissa jumped up again. "But, Uncle, when do we go to York?"

Maeve risked a glance up and met his gaze. His eyes were dark, unreadable, but her cheeks still burned from the intimacy of a moment before.

He answered, his absent frown back in place. "Tomorrow. I'll take you tomorrow if the weather holds clear."

With that, he strode out, and Maeve watched, her throat tight and her heart pounding in her chest as his dark-clad figure turned down the hall, heading toward his study.

She wanted to hide her face in her hands and never be seen again. She wanted to run out of the room and indulge the ridiculous tears that stung her eyes and teased to be let loose. She wanted . . . oh, she could not think of what she wanted. She had thought to breach his defenses, and had not given a single care to her own. She was well served, for she had opened herself to this folly, to this rush of feeling, to this impossible longing that ached in her chest like a fatal wound.

Clarissa's excited dancing around the room intruded on her thoughts, and Maeve tried to pull herself together.

"York! We're going to York tomorrow, and he's going to buy me a new piano. Oh, Miss Midden, you sing like an angel. You and Uncle were perfect together. Oh, wouldn't it be wonderful if he were to fall in—"

"No," Maeve said, so harshly that Clarissa stopped dancing and stood still, her smiles halted.

"But . . . don't you like . . . I mean, I know he is quite old, but you seem to—"

"Not another word," Maeve commanded, rounding on the girl, her breath coming too quickly and her feelings in tatters around her. "You must not even think of such an improper thing. Your uncle is a lord. He . . . that is, I . . . well, suffice it to say you should practice your scales, and leave other matters well enough alone. Now, if you will excuse me, I have a letter to write."

With that, Maeve hurried out before she lost all control. Oh, why had Clarissa said anything? Of course he would not fall in love with her. Even if he could, it would only lead to her having to reveal her past, and she could not . . . would not do that. She could not even bear the thought of it. So she ran to her room to hide herself and rebuild her own defenses. And she vowed never again to try to undo the walls around another person's heart.

They left for York the next morning with the day a touch cloudy, but no threat of rain in the white puffs that floated gently across the blue sky. Maeve marveled that she could act as if nothing at all had happened, and she would not let herself think about what it had cost her to recover her poise and calm demeanor. She had prided herself on her armor, and it worried her now to find that what she had taken for steel looked to be rusted through.

The colonel was as organized and efficient as if he were setting out for Spain again. He had the carriage ready and gleaming, refreshments lashed to the boot, and two footmen in smart green livery to ride on the rear seats outside the coach.

"Ducal style," he had joked to her.

It quite impressed Maeve as just that.

Clarissa waved to her mother, who leaned from an upper-story window and shouted down items that were not to be forgotten, including the latest novels at the lending library, ribbons and hat trimmings, two yards of muslin, and a tour of the ancient minster for Miss Midden.

Lord Rothe finally signaled to the liveried coachman, who cracked his whip and the four horses drawing the closed carriage pulled away from Rothe House.

Maeve realized as the coach swung out of the gates, with Clarissa wide-eyed and staring out the window, that a journey of nearly three hours now stretched before them until they arrived in York. So, to amuse Clarissa, Maeve began to recite the facts that tended to accumulate in any governess's mind. She had read that York was the only city in England, other than London, whose chief magistrate was honored with the title of Lord, and that the city had the benefit of twelve aldermen, two sheriffs, eight chamberlains, twenty-four councilmen, and a town clerk. At this point Clarissa began to yawn, so Maeve pulled out the story she had heard of how a certain Mrs. Thornton had ridden in and won, not once but twice, the races at York. That set Clarissa off on a wish to also ride a race, a thought quelled with a stern glance from Lord Rothe.

Maeve then offered up the safer topics of historic details about the minster, which she had read was fifty feet longer than Westminster Abbey, and York's history, including mention of the battle that had been fought at Marston Moors during the Civil War.

"They say nothing will grow amid the trees at Cromwell's Gap," Clarissa chimed in, turning her attention to the topic with ghoulish delight, "because of the royalist blood which once drenched the ground."

Lord Rothe frowned. "Nothing grows between the trees because precious little sun reaches the ground. Miss Midden, do you mean to instruct us this entire journey? I had thought this would be something of a holiday for everyone."

Which is why you face it with such grim determination, Maeve thought, but she only answered with meek acquiesce.

Andrew decided that he was an idiot.

He had been embarrassed yesterday when he had found himself tongue-tied and witless after that damned duet. Why had he ever allowed Clarissa to talk him into it? How was he ever going to excuse his behavior, or even explain it? He did not understand what had happened in that heart-stopping instant when his stare had locked with Maeve's yesterday in the music room.

So he blamed Clarissa, and he blamed the music.

His father had been a wiser man than Andrew had ever thought, for the damn music had always been what had made him dream and idle his way through life. Turning his back on it had been necessary for Andrew to embrace the military life. Now he had no room for it. A lord did not go about singing duets with his niece's companion, no matter how pretty she looked when she sang and gazed up with her face alight and her eyes dancing and . . .

Oh, good God, he was well past the years of infatuation, and he knew better than to take seriously any woman's smiles. Dorothy had taught him well about that, at least, for she'd had nothing but smiles and sweetness for him—and then for his brother when next he looked around. No, Miss Midden had done nothing but enjoy the music, so he was damned if he would make anything more of it than that.

He folded his arms and allowed the rest of the journey to pass watching Maeve and Clarissa idle the time with a traveling game of chess.

They arrived in York in good time, and Maeve found it a relief to step out of the carriage. In truth, she was not a good traveler. Closed carriages had the tendency to leave her head aching and her stomach spinning. However, the weather had been warm enough today that no one had objected when she let the window down on her side of the carriage, and the fresh air had made the trip bearable.

Relief washed through Maeve as she took the hand of a footman and stepped down into the cobbled yard of the posting house in York. She stood still a moment to stop that dreadful sensation of the world rocking, just as the carriage had. Around her, stable boys hurried forward to strip the harness away from the sweating bay geldings and lead them away to be brushed down and watered.

She took a deeper breath, feeling better, and glanced about. The inn was an old one, with a courtyard for carriages, and half-timbered house and stables. Clarissa had wandered to the back kitchen door of the inn to coo over a tumble of kittens that lay in a basket. Lord Rothe had stepped to the side to talk to the landlord, a portly man with not a hair on his head.

A groom led a saddled horse from the stables, and Maeve glanced at the showy chestnut, immediately thinking that its owner must set more store in his appearance than in his comfort, for the animal pranced nervously, and was too thin in the chest to be a pleasant ride.

Then a man stepped into the yard from the stable, his hat at a rakish angle, showing a flash of blond hair that gleamed like a newly minted guinea. His blue coat fit tightly over narrow shoulders, and his wasp-waist had to be formed by a corset's tug. He turned away abruptly, as if someone behind him had called to him, but a glimpse of his narrow face and aquiline nose had been enough.

Could it be . . . was it . . . Vincent?

Maeve's heart caught in her throat. *Oh, please, God, do not let it be him*, she prayed, harder than she had prayed for anything in her life. Not here. Not now.

She could hear Clarissa laughing over the kittens and asking her uncle if she could take one home. She could hear the colonel caution her that she would have to learn to care for the animal, and then ask the innkeeper if the kittens were for sale. But Maeve's world telescoped to the man in the blue coat as he began to turn and face her.

She could not breathe. She could not move. All her will focused in on making this not be Vincent.

Then he turned and looked directly at her.

Nine

It was not him.

Stunned relief coursed through Maeve, and she realized with lightheaded giddiness that of course it could not be him. He would have been nine years older, not this young gentleman's age. Somehow, in her mind, she had never aged Vincent from nine years ago. She watched the fellow toss a copper coin to the groom and then swing up on his flashy horse and ride away.

She pulled in a shaky breath. Her thoughts were spinning like a thrown cartwheel, and her knees threatened to give out like candles in a hot summer. The world seemed to narrow until it took all her will to focus on the gentleman who was now riding away. Her heart pounded against her chest, louder than the hoofbeats of the departing horse, and a rush of noise filled her ears. It was as if everything inside her had been poised for flight, to run and hide, and now there was no need for such action; her body did not seem to know what to do.

Then she realized that someone was calling her name. She looked up into Lord Rothe's scowling face.

Andrew decided in an instant that Maeve looked unsettlingly like a young recruit after a baptism by blood in a major skirmish. Pale-faced, a sheen upon her forehead and with a terrifying, empty look in her eyes, she swayed slightly, holding on to the carriage door with a fisted grip. He couldn't begin to imagine what had given her such a shock.

"Miss Midden, are you all right?" he demanded sharply.

It was a damned silly question, but he wanted her to focus her mind upon giving him a reply.

"Yes, I think so," she said, her voice small and wavering. She let go of the carriage and tried to straighten. Instead, she turned a ghastly white and started to sink to the ground.

He caught her as her knees buckled. She looked up at him, surprise replacing the empty shock on her face.

"I don't understand. I never faint."

Relief surged through him at seeing the color start back to her cheeks. Her body was still reacting to some over-powering distress, but if she could sound that put out, she must be starting to recover.

"Of course not," he said, and then swung her up in his arms, easily lifting her slight form as he called out, "Landlord, be quick, man. I need a private parlor for the lady."

She was the merest slip of a girl, as light as a feather quilt in his arms. Her head rested against his shoulder, and her damnable bonnet poked and scraped his face, but the rest of her was all softness. He cradled her closer, wanting to shelter her without even knowing why, or what it was that she needed to be sheltered from.

She did not protest his high-handed treatment, and her passivity triggered a raw, twisting fear in him. What the devil had pulled the barb from her tongue and the steel out of her spine?

The innkeeper led the way inside the dark inn with its narrow, shallow stairs worn by centuries of booted feet. He opened the door to a small parlor, and Andrew had to duck his head to enter the low-ceilinged room with walls framed by age-blackened timbers.

Clarissa followed behind, asking repeatedly if she could do something, a kitten still clutched in her arms and honest worry tight in her voice.

Andrew lay Maeve down upon a worn velvet-covered settee before an unlit fireplace. She tried to sit up at once, so he put a hand on her shoulder to keep her still, and then he sat down on the edge, the settee creaking underneath him, so that she could not get up again without colliding into him.

"Landlord, bring up some brandy," he ordered, already starting to untie Maeve's bonnet. "Clarissa, fetch water and a cloth."

Clarissa and the innkeeper both jumped to obey, and Andrew was left alone with Maeve.

"Now, miss, would you care to tell me what the devil happened out there?" he demanded.

Maeve put a hand to her head, which had started to pound, and realized that her bonnet was missing. That brought her surroundings into sudden focus.

She lay in a clean, sparsely furnished room. There were no fresh flowers on the mantel, and the only decoration on the wall was a print of a sailing ship. She frowned at the odd angle of everything, then realized that she was lying down, and the colonel was sitting next to her, staring at her with a very harsh scowl.

"What happened?" she repeated, her thoughts still scattered and sluggish. It all rushed back in an instant— the man in the yard, her fear, her relief, her light-headedness. And she knew equally as fast that she could not answer him with a lie, but she could not bear the shame of the truth if her answers led him to ask even more questions. She offered instead a speculation; "Perhaps it was *coup de soleil*?"

"*Coup de* . . . ? Miss Midden, the sun does not strike anyone that hard in Yorkshire. Now, you may tell me what happened, or I shall send for a doctor so that I may have my answers from him."

"Oh, please do not," Maeve said with forceful sincerity. "I am so sorry to have caused all this fuss. I thought . . . it was just a shock I had."

"A shock? Miss Midden, you looked as if you had seen your own ghost walking. I think you owe me a little more explanation that that."

She did owe him at least some explanation, and she could see from the look in his eyes and the set line to his mouth that he would worry her to death until she did give him some answer.

"I thought I saw someone . . . someone I had not hoped to see again in this lifetime. Only it was not him."

Andrew frowned down at her. He heard the hesitation in her voice, and the strain. *Someone I had not hoped to see again in this lifetime.* Did that mean she had loved and lost someone in the war, or did it mean someone she hated enough to wish never to see again in this life? A dozen questions clamored in his head—who was this fellow, what had he been to her, why did she not hope to see him again? However, he glanced at her pale face, at her hand which still trembled, and he said nothing more. He would not tease her for answers now, but he would have his answers someday, he vowed.

She edged up on one elbow, then seemed to realize that to sit up further she would have to press her body against his. Her cheeks flamed, and she lowered her stare to where his leg pressed against hers. He knew he ought to move away, but a reluctance to leave her kept him in place beside her. It was nonsense, this desire to shield her. She was a competent woman who had obviously looked after herself for years, but he could not forget how she had felt in his arms—so tiny, so delicate, so warm and vital.

Maeve swallowed the dryness in her mouth and wished

that she could faint again, or that the world would open up and engulf her. Anything to remove her from the temptation of being so close to him. She wanted his arms around her again so badly that she ached with the need for him. Lord, the last thing he needed was a woman clinging to him as if her life depended upon it.

"Are you better now?" he asked.

She nodded, unwilling to trust her voice, for fear it would be husky with desire and betray her.

He stood and helped her to sit upright, but he hovered so close beside her that his concern for her set her own nerves on edge. Oh, why had she ever agreed to come to York? She had known that this was the danger of going out into the world again. More than ever she needed a country house in which she could bury herself—forever.

The innkeeper returned with brandy and two glasses, which he set on the table under the far window. Then he bowed himself out. The colonel filled one glass half full and the other to the brim. He thrust the half-full glass at her and ordered, "Drink."

She accepted the brandy and was ashamed to see her hand quiver as she clutched the glass. She swallowed the bitter-smelling liquid, then wrinkled her nose as it seared its way down her throat and flowed out to tingle on her skin.

"How do you gentlemen drink this for pleasure?" she asked, her face screwed up against the biting taste.

"It's meant to be sipped and savored, not tossed back as if you'd grown up in a distillery."

Maeve averted her face, but not before Andrew saw a spasm of pain cross her countenance. He had meant his comment as a jest, some way to break the tension that had settled between them, but he now realized that its humor was too harsh for anyone who might be ashamed of their origins. He also realized that his voice had carried the edge of his temper. Lord, what right had he to be

angry? What did it matter that she'd been watching some
fellow and mistaken him for someone she'd once known?
His jaw tightened as the thought rankled him anew, and
he knew it was only his pride that lay behind his irritation.
He had been stung at the thought that there might be
some man in her past who had meant so much to her.

Who had she never hoped to see in this life again?

He cleared his throat and buried his feelings deeper.
"I'm not sure you should be jaunting about York today."

She looked up at him, and their eyes met. There was
in her gaze such a lost expression that he took a step
toward her, unaware of the action, needing only to close
the distance between them, wanting only to—

"I have the cloth," Clarissa said, bursting in.

Andrew turned toward her, ready with a sharp reminder
that she had been brought up to enter rooms like a lady
with a polite knock first. At the sight of Clarissa's eyes
gone wide with trepidation, he bit back his words. *My
God, she's afraid of me. Afraid of my temper.*

She covered her fear in an instant, her eyes flashing
with a dare for him to rebuke her.

He glanced once at Miss Midden's lowered head, wondering if she too feared his temper, as she had a right to
after his treatment of her today. Then he looked back at
Clarissa, who still stood in the doorway, an abundance of
flannel balanced in her hands. "Miss Midden felt faint,
Clarissa. She does not need her arms and legs and the
rest of her bound up like one of the ancients from Egypt."

His voice sounded rusty as he spoke, and he hoped he
had not laced too much sarcasm into his words.

With a fleeting smile, Clarissa flopped down on the
settee next to Maeve and offered her one of the cold com-
presses. "I brought several cloths, for they always get hot
and then they are horrid. There, doesn't that feel better?"
she asked, pressing one to Maeve's forehead.

Maeve felt an almost hysterical urge to laugh.

Clarissa's timing had either rescued her from one of life's most embarrassing moments or had interrupted . . .

She stopped herself and wondered just what had been interrupted. She glanced up at his lordship. He had turned away and had walked over to stare out one of the mullioned windows. He was frowning as usual, as remote and cold as ever, his dark eyes unreadable. She had thought for an instant that she had seen something else in his eyes, some spark of . . .

But, no, she might have imagined it. Or mistaken anger for some other feeling. He had probably only been about to issue more orders—he was very good at that—and she really should not read anything more into the situation than was there on the surface. She knew the danger of letting herself believe in illusions made by her heart's wishing.

"Thank you, dear," Maeve said, removing the compress and putting it with the others. "Why don't you leave these on the table there, with the brandy?"

"Brandy? Do I get a glass as well? It was quite shocking for me to see you carry Miss Midden into the inn that way, Uncle." Clarissa fixed an expectant stare on Lord Rothe.

"You may have a lemonade or some milk," he said, turning back to them.

Clarissa wrinkled her nose. "Thank you, but milk would make me ill on the way home. But you are not ill any longer, are you, Miss Midden?"

The plea in Clarissa's voice and eyes made Maeve sit straighter. She would not allow her problems to deny Clarissa this treat. "Of course I am not. I shall just—"

"You shall just stay here and rest." Lord Rothe strode away from the window to set down his glass upon the table.

Maeve started to protest, but Lord Rothe cut her off,

saying, "I think Clarissa and I can manage to buy out the shops in York on our own."

The pout that had been forming on Clarissa's rosebud lips disappeared into a brilliant smile. "Really? May we?" An unexpected frown descended on Clarissa's brow as she turned to Maeve. "But won't you be lonely here all on your own? Oh, I know—Jane can keep you company. That's what I'm naming the kitten, for she is a clever little thing, quite like my best friend in school. And she can keep you company."

Clarissa hurried out, her running steps carrying back to them from the uncarpeted wooden stairs. Maeve thought that the child really must learn to contain such exuberance before she appeared in London society, which expected docile misses.

Then she turned back to Lord Rothe, ready for battle again. She could not neglect her duties, and she could not help but worry that if she allowed him and Clarissa go out together they would come back with daggers drawn.

"Really, Lord Rothe, I am quite able to accompany you," she said, trying to sit straighter, but not daring to stand lest she spoil her words by starting to wobble.

He cocked one eyebrow and surveyed her critically.

Maeve decided he must have used that look during military parades to make lowly soldiers aware of every wrinkle in their uniforms. That look might also have reduced a woman with more sensibility to confused blushes, but Maeve lifted both of her eyebrows and stared back at him, refusing to be cowed.

The hint of a smile lit his dark eyes. "If you faint again on me, I must haul Clarissa back home without her so much as poking her nose into one store, and then I should not have a moment's peace in my house for months to come."

"So you claim selfish reasons for your actions?" she

asked, skeptical of his excuse. "You are not doing this out of consideration for me?"

"I have a reputation as a tyrant to my family to protect, Miss Midden. Since I have said you will stay here and rest, you must do so or I risk undermining my authority."

He spoke lightly, the mockery of himself strong in his voice and one dark eyebrow cocked. She was not mistaken, however; he was being kind to her.

"What's more, you will ask the innkeeper for anything you desire. Clarissa and I shall return at two for some refreshment before we set off for home. Is that understood?"

Maeve smiled a little and relented. Her worry over how he and Clarissa would get on was still there, but he seemed determined to go out with his niece, and equally determined to be in a good mood about it. Perhaps the time together would actually serve to make uncle and niece better known to each other.

"I shall try not to drink all the brandy while you are gone," Maeve said, her tone dry.

Andrew relaxed, relieved that she had not taken his bungled joke of earlier so hard that she could not turn it back on him now. He started to frame an apology for his earlier thoughtless words, but his mind went blank. Somehow, it all knotted up inside him until none of the things he wanted to say could come out.

Clarissa rescued him again, bouncing in to leave the small, fuzzy, gray Jane on Maeve's lap before she linked her arm through his and coaxed him out of the room.

It was a relief, in truth, to be left alone, Maeve thought, glancing down at Jane. The poor creature sat trembling, her fur sticking out, her eyes huge with fright as she looked around at these new surroundings. Maeve ran a finger down the soft fur and ticked under the small creature's chin until Jane looked up.

"I know exactly how you feel, being taken from your

family and left on these strange shores, but it will be all right." She cuddled the kitten close, soothing her cheek against the downy gray fur. "We must always believe it will be all right."

Maeve told herself that several times before she lay down and closed her eyes and tried to forget all the memories—the guilt, the pain, the shame—that had come back to her from nine years ago.

Someone was pulling on her hair.

Maeve opened her eyes and stared into two grayish blue orbs inches away. Jane the kitten batted at Maeve's hair again, and Maeve sat up with a start. The kitten leapt away and buried herself behind a pillow.

Wondering how long she had slept, Maeve put a hand up to her loose hair. It was still daylight, but she had never been good at judging the hour and there was no clock in the room. She got up. There was no mirror in the room either, but a glance around brought to her notice the brandy tray. It was a dull silver metal, but it would help her make herself presentable.

She propped the tray on the mantel, and it gave back a good enough image to show that Jane had torn apart the smooth braid she usually wore wrapped into a tight chignon in back. Loose curls hung about her face in frivolous abandon. She glanced down at her dress and smoothed its wrinkles, but they popped back as soon as her hands had passed over them.

She looked, she decided, as if she had slept in a trunk.

Clarissa's high chattering voice and a heavy step on the stair announced the return of her charge and her employer.

"Oh, they would come back now," Maeve cursed, trying to smooth back her hair again, the curls slipping through her fingers as she turned to face the door.

Clarissa came in, glowing with smiles and endless stories of what they had seen and done and bought. She had a shawl for Lady Rothe, and fabric for a dress for Miss Midden, and Uncle Andrew had ordered her a grand piano from William Stodart in London, although he had been heartless enough to deny her the fortepiano carved with Nubians holding up the body and painted with an Italian scene and gilt throughout.

Lord Rothe gave Maeve one glance—a frown—and then turned his attention to ordering refreshments. He seemed distracted, Maeve thought, for he had no rebukes concerning her appearance. Self-consciously she smoothed her hair again.

"Oh, do not push back the curls," Clarissa said, batting at Maeve's hair in much the same fashion as Jane had. They make you look ever so much younger."

"I'm not supposed to look younger," Maeve answered, amused and flattered despite her efforts not to be. "I'm supposed to look stern, so that I can quell chatter such as yours, miss, with a single glare."

Clarissa laughed. "You may quell my chatter with some tea, please, Miss Midden. I am positively parched. Unless I might have some brandy?" She threw a saucy, coy look over her shoulder at her uncle.

Maeve tensed with worry that Lord Rothe would be too sharp in stemming Clarissa's high spirits, but he smiled at his niece with a warmth in his eyes that Maeve had never before seen.

"Do you know, Clarissa, your mother used to look at me just so," he said, his voice softening with memory. Then the warmth iced over as if a North Sea wind had blown into the room. "And if I ever see you trying such tricks on any man young enough to be susceptible to them, you may be sure I will lock you away until you learn to behave yourself."

Clarissa bit her lower lip, subdued for a moment, but

then brightened. "Jane, there you are, hiding behind that pillow." She swept up the small kitten and turned to her uncle. "I am going to fetch Jane some milk. And I don't use tricks on anyone!" she shot out before sweeping out as dignified as a duchess.

Maeve glanced up at Lord Rothe. "She really does not mean to flirt so shamelessly, you know. I don't even think she is fully aware of the effect of her beauty, yet."

"That is not a recommendation. Her mother did the same thing. Went around, her head in the clouds, breaking half the hearts in the county."

"Yours as well?" Maeve asked, then bit her lip, ashamed that she had let the thought slip into spoken words.

He had been pouring a glass of brandy and now he paused, and looked at her. He hesitated a moment, then said, his tone flippant, "Do you know your English poets, Miss Midden? There's one who speaks to me—'my ragges of heart can like, wish and adore/But after one such love, can love no more.' "

She recognized the quote and could not help asking, "And what of Donne when he said, 'A naked thinking heart, that makes no show/Is to a woman, but a kinde of Ghost.'? Could it be, perhaps, that Lady Rothe did not know you loved her?"

He swirled the brandy in his glass, staring at the amber liquid, his expression distant as if he looked back into the past. "Oh, she knew. Enough to accept my proposal in private, if not in public. She thought better of it when I told her I was bound for the army. I could not, in any honor, hold her to that promise then. The army's no life for a woman. But I will not have Clarissa learning those kinds of tricks to play on a man."

Worry for him knotted inside Maeve. He had no idea, she realized, that he was looking at Clarissa and seeing someone else. He saw the image of the woman he had once loved, and that could only bring grief to everyone in the family. Something had to be done.

"If you honestly mean that," she said, her skin hot and the words burning inside her, "then you had best let her know that you do not hold her responsible for what happened between you and her mother."

He stared at her, both his eyebrows raised with haughty astonishment. "I hold . . . ? Just what the devil do you mean by that?"

"My lord, you seem to have made an excellent start today to come to know Clarissa. However, it seems to me that you still act as if she is her mother . . . and she is not."

"Of course she's not. But like mother . . ."

"Like daughter? You will certainly encourage her to follow her mother's examples if you refuse to recognize her own qualities. I know much about that from my own father's misguided efforts to mold my character," she said, the memories bitter of her own upbringing. "You must see that Clarissa believes you are strict with her and do not allow her any freedoms because you want some form of revenge against her mother for her rejection. Clarissa doesn't look at your actions and see that you are trying to keep her from becoming . . . well, that you are trying to keep her from unintentionally hurting others."

She had spoken rapidly, the words tumbling out, but now she bit down on her lower lip. The force of her feelings had taken her past what was beyond wise, or beyond her place as either a governess or a companion. She smoothed her dress again, and tried to smooth over her feelings, but she felt as if a lock had been turned inside her and whatever had been behind that sealed door must now come out. She could only try to direct it as best she could.

He stared at her, his expression as shocked as if she had slapped him. "That's absurd."

He looked so appalled by her idea that she found it difficult to continue to meet his gaze, so she focused again on smoothing the wrinkles from her gown. "It may sound absurd when spoken aloud, but thoughts always seem insidiously reasonable when they echo in those empty spaces in the mind. Clarissa has rather too much empty space around her. She is very much alone in Rothe House, despite my company. She has time to imagine almost anything."

She heard his glass slam against wood. She looked up to see him stride to the window, his hands folded behind his back, his profile to her. The pulse beat near his jaw, and his scowl had deepened so much that she did not dare say another word. Was he angry with her for speaking so bluntly, or with himself because he recognized the truth in her words?

Her body quivered with nervous dread at what his reaction might be. She had seen his temper, but she had never before felt exposed to it, for always there had been the armor of her position between them. She had stepped out of that armor today. Self-consciously she thrust back her shoulders, braced for the worst, but hoped she had not been mistaken in believing that he was a man who valued the truth highly.

Ah, well, perhaps her whole purpose at Rothe House was simply to tell everyone what they least wanted to hear and then go away. If that was the case, she could only hope that he dismissed her on the spot for her impertinence, rather than rip into her with his temper.

Clarissa came back into the room, smiling and hugging her kitten, and Maeve glanced up, worried that the girl would unwittingly draw his lordship's anger. The girl hesitated at once, her expression turning wary as she glanced from Maeve to Lord Rothe.

His lordship glanced at them. His scowl lessened, and the snapping anger left his black eyes. "Well, miss, have you fed your kitten? Where do you think they've hidden our lunch?"

His words came out clipped, so controlled that they sounded unnatural. But, for once, Clarissa acted with a wisdom beyond her years and did not comment. She picked up on his questions, answering them politely, and Maeve breathed out a deep sigh of relief.

But then he shot her a dark look, and she knew that this was still not settled between them. She had disturbed his orderly world, and he would not rest until he had set everything back in its place. Oh, when would she learn not to meddle in affairs that were really none of her concern?

The journey home passed with no other incidents. Clarissa chattered about pianos and shops, and Maeve tried to remain interested in the conversation so as to spare Lord Rothe from being pestered by too many questions. He remained silent and thoughtful the entire trip. The sky darkened as the carriage took them home, their pace brisk enough so that they arrived before the moon had risen and with just enough of the lengthening daylight to help them into the house.

It was then that Lord Rothe turned to Maeve and asked abruptly, "Would you come with me to my study for a moment? You may go on, Clarissa, and change for dinner."

A troubled frown pulled Clarissa's dark brows together in a fair imitation of her uncle's expression. She hesitated in the hallway and shot a glance at Maeve. "A word? Whatever about?"

"Why don't you go up to your mother and show her Jane, and her shawl?" Maeve said, trying not to let her own nervousness show. Oh, Lord, what did he want to talk to her about? About her dismissal? Would he be dreadfully cold with her, or loud and angry? She hoped not the latter. She had not the nerves left in her today to deal with the latter.

Clarissa hesitated a moment longer, shooting a look from Maeve to her uncle, but the footmen began to bring in her purchases of the day, and the task of ordering which packages went where distracted the girl.

Maeve turned to face Lord Rothe. She felt slightly ill, her head still ached, and her mouth was dry and still tasted foul from the brandy. It was vastly unfair, she realized as she took in the withdrawn and set look to his face. Now, it mattered to her whether she stayed or not. She had tangled herself up with Clarissa, and with him, and even with Dorothy's life. She did not want to leave. For the first time, the power of his being able to dismiss her, to send her away, stung her like the crack of a whip.

He was within his rights to ask her to go, of course. She had presumed to criticize how he dealt with his niece. She had interfered in his private life. She still had the ten pounds he had given her, but he would be within his rights to turn her out without a farthing more, forcing her to make her way back to York as best she might. Or perhaps he would simply demand an apology.

Only she could not apologize. She would not. Not to earn her position back, and not even to secure the comfort of a place in his carriage back to York where she could catch the mail coach. No, she had been wrong to speak, but her words had been nothing but the truth—a much needed truth, in fact. If he could not, or would not, recognize that, then she would travel as cheaply as she could back to Bath. She would find a new position as soon as she could, and she would have to pray that her savings outlasted her wait.

He led the way to his study, pausing to hold the doors open for her, saying nothing. Her heart had dropped to her shoes by the time he showed her into the book-lined room, which should have looked comforting with the lit fire and candlelight, but which merely seemed ominous to her. She wished very much that they had simply had this out back in York. She would have been spared the need of making the trip twice.

She blinked back a sudden rush of tears as thoughts of how she would have to say her good-byes to everyone swamped her for an instant. She tried to tell herself that these were simply tears of frustration and anger, but her willful heart refused to believe that logical explanation.

"I suppose you know what I want to say to you?" he asked, pacing between his desk and the bookcases on the opposite side of the room.

She nodded, then realized that he was not looking at her but was staring into the fire. She took a moment to compose herself, to take a firm grip on her reticule; then she said, her voice calm and not trembling in the way that her insides shook, "Yes, and I would at least hope you will allow me to leave tomorrow morning, rather than tonight."

He turned to stare at her, and the firelight must have played tricks, for it seemed to her that she caught a flash of panic in his eyes, but it must only have been a glimmer of light.

"You would like . . .? Why the devil are you leaving?" he demanded, his voice sharp and not the least bit panicked.

"Because . . . well, aren't you . . . don't you intend to give me notice?"

He dragged a hand through his hair and then ran it over his face. He looked tired suddenly, as if he was ready to drop where he stood.

She started toward him, unable to stop the instinctive response, but then her years of hard schooling took over and she stood still, waiting for his answer.

"Miss Midden, I apologize most heartily for making an utter mull of everything. I seem not to know how to even talk to people these days without the words coming out like a command or a rebuke. I think I have forgotten how to be civilized." He looked up at her, his eyes unguarded, his hands spread, palms up. "Miss Midden, will you help me please to remember what it is to be part of a family again?"

Ten

She stared at him, dazed, the words she'd had ready to say no longer necessary. She had prepared herself for a confrontation, and this abrupt change sparked confusion first, and then indignant outrage. He was not supposed to act like this. He was supposed to take her apart with that icy control of his. He was supposed to act like an abrupt, commanding military man, not as if . . . well, as if he needed her. He needed no one.

And what was she to do now? How could she answer him?

Tears born of frustration and confusion sprang up to burn the backs of her eyes and blur her vision. She dared not wipe at them for fear that more would gather. Oh, why did he have to pick this moment to be so unpredictable? Why could he have not have waited until she'd had a good night's sleep instead of a tiresome, exhausting day behind her?

"My lord," she said, her voice not quite steady, "I said things to you today that I should not have. After that, you *must* want me to leave."

"Must I really?" he asked, a fraction of a smile softening his mouth.

That tentative, hopeful smile undid her.

She gave up suddenly, anger and irritation draining out of her. Those emotions had simply been a last defense against this house—against him. She was caught, firmly

and fast. She had made the mistake of caring—and someday she would have to leave them all. If not today, then
soon.

And how much worse would it be to bear then?

The tears began to flow before she could stop them.

She wiped her damp face with her gloved hands and
tried to sniffle them back, but the tears would not stop.
She turned aside, hating this unseemly display, embarrassed by her lack of control, and torn utterly by her need
to leave before she was even more deeply involved.

It was herself, not him, who had made an awful mess
of things here. Could he not see that?

"Maeve," he said, striding across the room, his boots
soft on the carpet and then hard on the wood until he was
beside her, taking her hands in an uncertain grip, brushing
her cheek with his broad thumb. "Please do not . . ."

She found a large linen handkerchief in her hands. She
took it because it was something to bury her face in so
that she did not have to meet his stare. He must be disgusted with yet another emotional female who burst into
tears for no sensible reason whatsoever.

Then he was leading her to one of the leather chairs
and making her sit down.

She blew her nose into his handkerchief and wiped her
eyes, and tried to gather her wits. "It seems to be my day
to do everything I never do," she said, sniffing and trying
to remain composed. "I never cry. Honestly, I don't."

His mouth twisted in a rueful smile and his eyes
warmed. "You have good excuse for tears today, between
what happened in York and my tactless blundering."

She fixed her stare upon the handkerchief that she was
knotting in her fists. She could not trust herself to answer
without another burst of waterworks. She felt as if someone had turned her inside out, putting all her feelings on
the outside where the air and light stung them raw. Was
she destined to always behave so foolishly?

Andrew watched the emotions play across her face—
the small wince of remorse as her mouth jerked tight, the
shadow of some past loss clouding her eyes, but she said
nothing. He did not like to be around women who cried.
Clarissa's theatrical sobs set his teeth on edge, and
Dorothy's silent tears had always flayed the guilt out of
him with every drop. But Maeve's misery cut into him
like a saber to the heart, leaving a clean, deep gash that
would not stop aching. He wanted to do something to
reassure her, to comfort her. She was not a woman who
would cry without cause. His hovering over her seemed
not to be helping, so he crossed to the chair opposite,
dragged it closer to her and sat down.

"You've had a tiring time today, and here I am teasing
you about taking on the impossible task of civilizing an
old soldier such as myself," he said, speaking lightly so
that she would not guess how shaken she had left him.
"My very lack of tact shows how badly your skills are
needed. However, consider yourself warned. I was the
bane of the duke's army—the only officer who had to
be commanded to attend the balls that Wellington was
so famous for. It was quite shameful, and the Peer himself told me that if I had not been such a good officer,
he would have shipped me home for being such a dull
fellow."

She gave him a wavering smile. "And how did you
answer that?"

"I told him it was a good thing that he could maneuver
as well on the battlefield as he could in the ballroom, or
I would have accepted those orders home."

She relaxed and her eyes warmed. His own shoulders
eased down as he saw the anxiety leave her expression.

"Come, Miss Midden, weren't you looking for a house
which could give you long-standing occupation? Don't
you see work enough to keep you busy here for the
ages?"

She was tempted. She watched him from lowered lashes and hesitated, held back by the last fragments of reason, which whispered that it would only be worse if she stayed for a year or two and then had to leave them.

Them? You mean him, don't you?

The truth lay in her as hard as iron and just as cold. She did not want to leave. But her life must someday take her away. Or would she stay and watch Clarissa marry, and perhaps Lord Rothe as well?

She clenched her fists and tried to ignore the pain that twisted inside her. She needed to make a rational decision, not one based on emotion. She had followed her heart once before, and it had led her into disaster. She had sworn never to again act without careful deliberation. But he was right—she was needed here. So could she stay?

And what will you do when the family goes to London for Clarissa's first season?

She winced as she thought of York and how badly she had acted there today. In London, how many times would she turn a corner and expect to see Vincent? How many times would she glimpse some dandy and fear for an instant that it was him? London was Vincent's haunt. For all its size and eminence, the fashionable four hundred kept to a small circle. Going there would be like going into the lion's den. She had not the courage to do that.

She wet her lips and began in a reasonable tone, "It is very kind of you—"

"I am not a kind person," he interrupted, a deep line appearing between his black eyebrows as he scowled at her.

After everything she had gone through today, she was not about to put up with being contradicted by him. "You are," she insisted. "You are also stubborn, and at the present frowning at me as if you wished you could use military discipline on me."

He put his fingers up to rub away the line between his eyebrows; then the edge of a smile pulled up the corner of his mouth. "I frown when I think. It's a habit that served me in good stead when I had a musical composition floating around in my head, for no one would dare interrupt me. And it continued to work to my advantage with my subordinates. I suppose it is also what causes Clarissa to flinch when I look in her direction."

"That and your tendency to bark orders at her and everyone else under your power. You and she are much alike, you know. You are both headstrong and believe you know better than anyone else."

"The difference is that I've learned to take orders, and I've learned how fallible I can be."

He got up and strode to the globe that stood near his desk. He spun it once, then turned toward her, his hands folded behind his back. "I fear I may be a hopeless case, but will you not at least try? I have no one else to call friend here, Miss Midden. Clarissa, as you point out, has cast me as the 'wicked guardian' in her own drama. Dorothy and I . . . we share too much history. And the servants . . . well, let us simply say they know their place, while I do not know mine. I was a bad student as a boy, and I expect I am no better now. My mind gets busy with a hundred other things. But I would stand in your debt if you could guide me at least a little of the way toward what I must become."

Warmth blossomed treacherously inside her at that thought. He had said she was his friend. What else might she become to him? She could not ignore the spark of hope that ignited. One could live without a good deal, she had learned, but one could not live without hope.

She glanced down at his handkerchief, now sodden and wrinkled, and she smoothed the embroidered crest. She looked up, her decision made.

"My lord, I find it difficult to believe that you lack

the nature of a gentleman, but I should be happy to oblige you. You've treated me very well, and I owe you the same courtesy in return."

She spoke with such stilted formality that Andrew's cravat tightened about his throat and he could not think how to answer her. He hated the stilted, posturing social graces. He'd always been bad with them—tongue-tied and awkward. Music had spoken for him for years, and then he'd taken to the coarse language of soldiers with a deep sigh of relief. He had hidden himself, he knew, away from this sort of thing. Good God, had he actually asked her to teach him about such things?

A hint of a mischievous smile lit her eyes and curved her mouth into an attractive bow, almost as if in invitation to laugh with her at these absurd requirements of civilization.

He started to relax, and then she added, "The only problem I foresee is when do you propose this . . . instruction might take place? I've already noted that you have little time to spend with your family, so how do you propose to find time for this?"

He frowned at her, then remembered her rebuke and consciously tried not to furrow his brow. He strode around his desk to his appointment book, saying, "Nonsense. I ought to at least be master of my own schedule."

She came over to stand beside him. "Yes, well, I see there is a weekly meeting with the head gardener marked in for every Friday. Perhaps that could be moved?"

"No. I cannot put that off. Meeks would be mortally offended if I did not listen to his complaints, approve his planting choices and express an interest in the kitchen garden."

"Ah, I quite understand. This is a large household to feed, and you cannot do without the kitchen garden. And of course you must meet with your steward in the mornings, but what about this appointment here on Thursday?"

"That's with the architect. I've put him off three times before, so I cannot move him again. He needs me to approve the supplies to refurbish the ruined wing. However, I've an inspection of the home farm I could delay."

"But that only provides one afternoon." She glanced up at him. "Do you think one afternoon would suffice?"

He met her serious gaze and thought, *You minx.* She was goading him, chiding him for filling his time with estate business, but, *damn it,* it was not as if he were trying to avoid his family. No, he simply . . . well, he simply had other pressing obligations. He closed his appointment book with a snap and a resolution to overlook her subtle hints that he should make time to see more of his niece and her mother. "There's only one option left."

"To abandon the idea?" she asked, her eyebrows lifting, her hands now folded primly before her.

"Not at all. To meet at an hour when we are both sure to have time. We shall meet at midnight."

She laughed. It was the first time he had ever seen her give an open laugh, and he found himself smiling in response, delighted at how her eyes danced and how her face lit with a soft glow.

"And shall we dance by the light of the moon as well?" she asked.

"My steps are probably as rusty as my sword, so that is another area you may polish. Clarissa would be mortified if I stood up with her at her first ball and then proceeded to trip over my own feet."

The amusement left Maeve's face as if stricken away, and irritation flashed in him. *Damn.* What the devil was it about the thought of society that so frightened her? Lord knew those affairs could be ordeals for anyone, but she seemed to have an extraordinary fear.

He got up and opened his appointment book again. He flipped open the inkwell, took up a trimmed quill, wet the tip in the ink and wrote, " 'Miss Midden, midnight.'

There. You are in the schedule now, Miss Midden. I expect you to be prompt. Tuesdays and Thursdays. Starting tonight."

Maeve stared at the bold writing in his appointment book. Writing always made something look far more real—far more daunting. She glanced up to the colonel—no, to Lord Rothe, she reminded herself. His dark eyes seemed unfathomable. His stern face with its harsh planes—the tan cheekbones, the strong jaw—seemed implacable.

She looked down again at the book, at his hand which rested beside the open page. He had long fingers that tapered at the tips. The backs of his hands were also long, and narrow. Sensitive hands. Nervous hands. At the moment, one long, elegant finger rubbed a small circle on the polished desk, the movement an unconscious betrayal of uncertainty. Sudden, unexpected comfort tingled on her skin. So he had his weak moments. He was not always so certain, so strong.

She glanced up at him again. He was as lost about this as she, and that somehow made it possible to go ahead with this ridiculous notion of teaching him the gentle arts.

"Very well. Midnight it is. And perhaps the witching hour will lend its own magic to this enterprise."

The clock on the mantel above the fireplace chimed for half past eleven in a maddeningly measured cadence. Maeve glanced at it, her hands quivering with anticipation as if she were meeting a lover, not her employer. This was far too much like a clandestine meeting for comfort, but it was also the most exciting thing that had happened to her in years. She knew she was only going to meet him to discuss the deportment of a lord, but she did not care about the excuse. She would hoard these hours with him against an uncertain future. She would give herself over to the pleasure of the present. She would simply enjoy his company.

It was madness. It could never go anywhere—a lord and a governess. Absurd.

And a sweet madness at that, her heart whispered.

Drawing a breath, Maeve bent her will toward stilling her erratic thoughts.

She sat on the edge of her bed, drawing a silver-backed horsehair brush through her unbraided hair. Was he pacing in his room? Would he even remember? Perhaps he would fall asleep and would not come?

You silly girl! You sound as absurd as Clarissa with her fancies.

She drew the brush again over the length of her hair. She should have cut it years ago to a sensible length, but she loved the sensuous feel of it. She loved the caress of its weight against her bare back when she dressed and undressed. And its colors told the history of her life, from the golden brown tips that marked its color as a girl to the dark cherrywood hues near her scalp that showed her more sober years as a governess. So many memories were woven in those shifting hues, like the flow of a dark river.

Sitting there brushing it made her think of times when she was a small girl and her own governess had pulled the silver-backed brush across it, telling her stories before she was tucked her into her own bed in her own house.

They were good memories. They made her forget her nerves. So she closed her eyes and tried to shut out the dragging minutes.

A knock on the door had her on her feet in an instant, her hand clenched around the brush, her hair swirling around her. "Who is it?"

The door creaked open, and Clarissa looked around the carved oak door. "May I come in?"

Without waiting for a reply, Clarissa slipped into the room. She had on a fetching nightcap, all lace and blue ribbons. A padded blue satin dressing gown lay open over a white cambric nightgown. She looked innocent as an angel—her eyes wide and guileless, her face serene—and that alone caused a tingle of suspicion to chase up Maeve's spine. Clarissa, she had learned, saved this face for when she was plotting something.

"What beautiful hair you have," Clarissa said, skipping in and then curling up on Maeve's bed. "I wish mine was dark; it's so much more fashionable."

Maeve folded her arms and studied the girl, in no way moved by this flattery. "You have lovely hair, my dear. Far more attractive than mine. And should you not be in your bed, getting your beauty sleep?"

Clarissa wrinkled her nose. "As if I could. It was a lovely day, was it not? I wish you had been feeling better so you could have come with us. Uncle Andrew let me buy anything and everything I asked for." She frowned. "But I don't think he was really paying attention to me at all. Mother says that gentlemen who agree with you are actually simply hiding their lack of interest. Do you think that's true?"

Maeve rose to put her brush back on the dresser next to her silver comb, the only things she had from her home. She did not want to talk about York, or what had happened there, so she answered, "Not always. But tell me, how is Jane settling? I hope you have not allowed her to shred your bed curtains with her claws."

"No. Not at all. Mrs. Henderson arranged a basket for her in my room, but she insists on hiding underneath the wardrobe—that is, Jane insists, not Mrs. Henderson." Clarissa let out a giggle at her own joke.

"You'll have to coax her out first thing. Mrs. Henderson will not appreciate it if Jane has an accident upon your rug."

"Oh, she won't. She is far too much the lady." Clarissa tucked her feet up, wrapped her arms around her legs and propped her chin on her knees. "Miss Midden, may I ask a personal question? I have been wondering something all day and I simply must know. Why did you faint? Did you see someone?" Her tone dropped to a low, dramatic note. "Did something happen?"

Maeve busied herself with the needless task of tidying her already tidy dressing table. She aligned her brush and comb, and began to push her hair pins into a small pile. "My dear, there are any number of embarrassingly silly reasons to faint, such as setting out on a journey on an empty stomach."

Glancing up, Maeve saw Clarissa's mouth take on a mulish pout. "You mean . . . do you mean to say you didn't . . . that the man wasn't . . ."

"What man?" Maeve asked, her throat tight with the fear that Clarissa's sharp eyes had seen too much today.

"Oh, you know—the fair-haired gentleman with the restive chestnut. He was quite dashing, although I think Papa would have said that gelding was just a touch light of bone."

A reluctant smile tugged on Maeve's lips. Only Clarissa could proclaim a man dashing and then turn practical about his taste in horseflesh. "You have been building a sand castle, Clarissa. I did not meet or see anyone I know in York."

It was not a lie, and Maeve had never felt stronger about withholding the details of this particular episode in her past, for if Clarissa knew, she might remake it into moonlit nonsense, and heaven only knew what other ideas such an incident might put into the girl's head.

Coming over to the bed, Maeve sat down next to Clarissa. "That gentleman with the chestnut horse—he was far too young to be . . . well, to be a close acquaintance of mine."

"Well, I'm glad of it. No, really. For your sake, for I

honestly do realize how awkward it would have been. I guess . . . well, I only wish . . ."

"What, my dear?"

"Well, I wish I had secrets to hide, but nothing ever happens to me worth keeping secret."

Smiling, Maeve pulled at Clarissa's nightcap. "If you wish to keep a secret, then you may keep it secret that you have been sneaking into my chambers so late, you naughty girl. Now, it's off with you to bed, or your tired eyes will reveal our wickedness."

"Oh, very well." Clarissa rose and started for the door, her feet dragging. Halfway there she stopped, turned and ran back to Maeve to hug her. "I am so glad you came. Whatever it took to get you here to us, I'm not sorry for it."

Maeve could not help but hug the girl back; then she held her away. "I do wish you would not make my life into something exotic and romantic. I would undo much of my past if I could, but if it meant that I would never meet you, then, my dear, I would do it again in a trice."

With a secret smile in her eyes, Clarissa squeezed Maeve's hands. "Then someday you simply must tell me how you fell in love and had your heart broken, and all the rest that brought you to us. But I know you're tired, so I won't tease you any more tonight. Good night, my dear Miss Midden."

Clarissa brushed her lips to Maeve's cheek and then flitted out the room, leaving Maeve bemused and just the faintest bit worried that someday perhaps Clarissa would learn the full story. Well, that would be one way to end her employment at Rothe House, but it would not be a pleasant method.

The clock chimed midnight, and Maeve gave a start. She was going to be late to meet the colonel. She put a hand up to her unbraided hair, but there was no use doing anything about that now. She would have to braid it as she went.

She grabbed her nightcap off the bed, glanced around the room to see if she had forgotten anything, then took up a candle and went out into the hall.

The night was warm with spring as she hurried on to the ruined wing, her slippers hushed against the hall carpet. Rain from that morning softened the air, and brought scents of fresh cut grass and warm earth.

At the doorway to the ruined wing, she stopped and put her candle down. She quickly braided her hair and tied it with a ribbon from her dressing gown pocket. Then she belted her gown tighter, picked up her candle and walked into the ruined room.

Eleven

A silver candelabra held up five white candles which cast a golden pool of light into the cavernous darkness. In the shadows, Maeve glimpsed the bare stone walls and the gaping holes where windows had once glinted; overhead, stars glittered like scattered embers. She took all this in at a glance, for it was the man who lay at the edge of the light who captured her attention.

Lord Rothe reclined on an Oriental carpet, his profile to her and his hands locked behind his head. The candlelight flickered over his profile, making his cheekbones seem higher, his face sharper. With his white shirt, buff breeches and dark looks, he seemed almost more like a pasha from some exotic land, or perhaps some dark fairy prince come to dance in the mortal world for a night.

Maeve hesitated, uncertainty flooding her. But he had heard the scuff of her slippers on the stone, and he turned away from his stargazing, rising up on one elbow as he did so, and Maeve stopped thinking.

He wore no cravat. His shirt hung open, white lawn framing hard muscle and a glimpse of his chest. His tan stopped at the curve of his throat, and just below, the faintest trace of dark hair wove a pattern of soft curls.

Maeve's heart lurched into her throat with an excited pounding. Into her mind flashed the image—the imagined feel—of being pressed against him, of her bare breasts brushing across those dark curls on his chest. She drew in a hot breath, the longing tight in her.

Then she shut her eyes. She must not think about these things. She had buried these sinful longings nine years ago when they had led her to her ruin. She would not allow them to rule her again. Only it would be harder this time, for now she knew where those urgings could lead.

She heard the scuffle of his clothing as he rose, and she opened her eyes. His brisk military stride banished his languor of the previous moment.

"Please, I wish you would not rise," she said, coming to meet him, trying to cover her pounding heart with a crisp step and her governess voice. "You looked so comfortable."

"You really must make up your mind, Miss Midden. Am I to be a boorish military man with no manners at all, or a civilized fellow who must make some effort to exert himself on behalf of others?"

She took a small risk and smiled up at him. "My lord, your title alone gives you license to do as you please. No one ever criticizes a lord's manners to his face. So you may put out your candle by throwing it across the room. You may apologize for the cook in someone else's house. You may even take up the habit of cursing as foully as a duke. The trick is to do so with the expectation that you are above censure."

"Do you imply I have excellent training for all that in my natural arrogance?" he asked lightly, handing her down to sit on a pillow. He bent to arrange the candelabra so the light did not shine too strongly upon them. "I assure you, that's anything but true. I have the habit of command, but I know what it is to do as my superiors order."

"Well, you will meet few superiors in society."

"Is that flattery?" Andrew asked, and then he had the pleasure of watching a blush creep into her cheeks.

He settled himself on the carpet with his back to the

wall, far enough from Miss Midden that she would not feel crowded by him, but close enough that he could enjoy the sight of her by candlelight.

He was not quite sure what was different about her tonight. Perhaps it was only the golden light, soft on her features, sparking fire in her eyes and color in her cheeks. Perhaps it was that her braid was not its usual tight rope, but lay over her shoulder, stray curls sliding out of the loose weave. Perhaps it was just that he was happy to have her company.

He had been tormenting himself with memories, with regrets for things that had happened and would never happen. *Why had Phillip died so young?*

Maeve's soft voice pulled him out of those thoughts. "Why so quiet, my lord?"

"My lord again, is it? It doesn't seem proper for the teacher to offer such deference to the student. Perhaps you might call me Andrew?"

"Well . . ."

"Come now. There's no one to overhear or disapprove, and I think we should be on more equal footing. The real question to settle between us now is where do we begin, for I have no notion how to start this reform."

She drew up her knees and hugged them to her. "Why don't you start by telling me more about your day in York with Clarissa? She said that you indulged her shamefully, and allowed her to buy anything she liked."

He gave a small, indifferent shrug. He did not care to talk about Clarissa, but if Maeve asked . . . "She did not demand diamonds or furs, so it was easy enough to oblige. In fact, it surprised me how little she demanded."

"It's only attention she wants. You know, she believes you did not even notice what she bought in York today."

He gave her a wry smile. "Meaning I did not flatter and praise every item she paraded for my inspection. She is a conceited baggage, and I was not about to make her more so. And why is it that all our discussions somehow end or begin with Clarissa as the topic?"

"We talk about her because she is what we have in common, sir."

"But is she all we have in common? If that's true, I must try harder to enlarge my interests," he said, his tone dry.

She smiled at this. "You had wider interests at one time, I believe. You had a love of music."

He glanced at her. She had taken her lower lip between her teeth, and she stared at him with worried eyes. Did she think her question too intimate? He studied her, searching for an answer. She had a curving mouth with a full lower lip, and he wondered briefly if he ran his thumb over it, would she set it free and would it feel as soft as a rose petal and would . . .

"Maeve," he said, sitting straighter and shaking off thoughts he had no right to entertain. "Music was not an interest. It was an obsession."

"But why do you not take it up again? As an interest this time? A hobby?"

He gave her a rueful smile and shook his head. She looked adorably serious with her nightcap slightly askew. But she had no idea what she was asking from him. "I cannot."

"Why ever not?" she said, as dogged as a terrier.

Yes, that was exactly what she was—his fierce terrier. Small of size, but boundless in spirit. When she sank her teeth into a problem, she would not let go unless rebuked for her impudence, and he had no such plans.

But what was he to tell her? He ran a hand through his hair. He did not want to talk about himself. Then he glanced at her. She stared back, her eyes focused intently on him, and it occurred to him that the price he must pay for luring her out of her deferential governess role would be answering her uncomfortable questions.

So he frowned and answered, his voice curt, "When I took up my commission, I promised my father I would never again touch a musical instrument. I would not write music, nor would I play. That oath still binds me."

Her eyes turned stormy gray. "How could he deny you something you loved so deeply? Was he heartless?"

He tried not to smile. He had not expected her to be angry for him. He could not remember a time when someone had felt moved to defend him.

As for the past, he lifted one hand to brush it aside. "No. Not heartless. Quite the opposite, for that vow most likely saved my life."

She waited, her expression expectant, and so he felt compelled to continue.

"You see, my uncle had served in the army, and I think he told my father much about his years there. I think my father knew that if I went to Spain with my head full of melodies and dreams, I would not have my attention on the job at hand. War is a nasty business, and an exhilarating one as well. Yet, between battles there are long spells of boredom. That's when a man can lose his edge. I saw it happen. A man would get a letter from home and he'd grow distracted. A few days later, he'd fall. I had to learn never to let my attention wander, and that was a difficult lesson for me."

"And what did it cost you to master such a skill? Lessons always come at a price—particularly those that require us to compromise some part of ourselves."

"Compromise?" he asked, a little touched by her concern for him. She seemed to take this so much to heart, as if it affected her personally. "Not quite the word for what I did. What is it the Bible says, that the boy must put aside the things of boyhood to become a man? I made a choice of my own free will, and I am happy to live with the promise I made."

Maeve looked at him, her chin lowered and her heart

troubled. He had made a difficult choice. She knew much about that. But what else had he lost when he had cut off that part of himself? Perhaps his choice had left him only with honor and duty, and now a title he did not want.

He smiled, though, and his black eyes glittered with wry amusement. "Honestly, you have been picking up Clarissa's desire to read tragedy in everyone else's life. I admit that sometimes I miss playing, but whatever used to inspire me with the need for it must have died from neglect, for the drive is not there. My mother used to say that talent needed to be tended like a delicate flower. She might have been right."

"What was she like—your mother?" Maeve asked, glad for a way to divert him from less happy memories.

His face softened, the lines falling out of the harsh planes, and his eyes warmed. Maeve noted the fine white creases around his eyes from squinting into the Spanish sunlight. One dark lock of hair had fallen over his forehead, and the slightest of smiles curved his mouth in the most inviting arch. Maeve's pulse skipped to a faster beat and her mouth dried. She ignored both and concentrated on what he was saying.

"Ah, my mother. She was a lady who adored music. I inherited that from her—though not her fair coloring. And she had the most beautiful voice. She taught me to play the harpsichord, the fortepiano, and the lute even. I was very much her son for the training, while Phillip belonged to my father, since he was to inherit the title."

"It sounds as if you adored her."

His face tightened. "I did. She died when I was ten."

He said it so casually, as if it had not mattered, but Maeve knew about what secrets could lie behind a controlled, careful tone. She knew about the need to hide the deepest hurts.

"At least you have memories of her," she said. "That must be lovely."

He frowned, and the line deepened between his eyebrows. "You say that as if you don't have such things."

"I don't. My mother died from complications brought on in childbirth, when I was four. I never knew her. But I used to make up stories about her. Outlandish stories, not unlike Clarissa's tales. And, unfortunately, I grew up a dreadfully spoilt child."

He hesitated, then put out a hand to touch her arm lightly. "I am sorry."

She felt the heat on her face, and her stare dropped to the intricate pattern on the carpet. "Please, don't be. My father more than overcompensated for the lack of two parents. If you think Clarissa willful, you would have thought me a monster. As the only girl in the house—and the only child—I got terribly accustomed to getting my own way in all matters."

"I see that is where you learned your bossy habits. But how did that lead you to becoming a governess? Did your father die and leave you penniless?"

She wiggled her left foot out of its slipper and dug her toes into the velvet pile of the carpet. The softness on her foot distracted her from the splinters of memories that lodged sharp in her chest.

"No. My father is still alive, but . . . we are estranged. And I . . . like you, I learned to put away the things of my youth."

For a moment the silence stretched taut between them. She dug her toes deeper into the carpet, down to the unyielding weave underneath. *Please do not ask me more,* she prayed. She did not want to lie to him, but she could not tell him the truth. She could not face the shame of seeing shock and perhaps revulsion come into his face if he ever learned about her past.

She risked a glance at him and found him watching her intently. She felt trapped and exposed, and could only repeat her silent prayer for a reprieve.

He looked away, then glanced back and gave her a small smile. "It's terribly rude of an employer to ask so many personal questions about his staff, is it not? I am afraid I never get that balance right between what is an interested question and what is prying."

He spoke lightly, making a jest of how personal his questions had been.

Relief flared in Maeve, but it was a bitter salvation. His words had also reminded her of their status. He was right to remind them both. She had forgotten that she was not in a position to afford the luxury of making another mistake with her life.

She slid her foot back into her slipper and managed to say with a smile, "Curiosity, when it comes with genuine concern, my lord, is always a forgivable fault. But I believe our discussion should center more on your family. It is them we aim to fit you to."

"Is that our aim?" he asked, his voice dropping to such a low tone that it echoed in her chest.

She met his gaze. His eyes had darkened with some emotion she did not recognize but which drew her closer to him as if he were pulling her to him with his hands. She leaned forward without realizing what she was doing. His stare searched her face, and she had to part her lips to draw in an unsteady breath.

The sputtering of a candle recalled her from folly when her mouth was but inches away from his.

She looked away at once, her face hot and her thoughts clamoring like church bells sounding an alarm. What was she doing? It was the hour. Yes, that was it. She was tired. That was all.

It was time for her to go.

"I think the candles are nearly burnt out, my lord . . . I mean, Andrew," she said, rising to her feet. The effort to rise gave her as good excuse as any why the blood should rush to her face, and reason to busy her hands smoothing her gown and straightening her nightcap.

He rose as well, but he took one of her hands, forcing her to stay. She could not look up to meet his gaze and so she stared at his hand, watching his fingers close around hers, trying not to move her touch across his hot skin in response. Her heart hammered against her chest like a cannon against castle walls.

"We have an appointment this Thursday next," he reminded her. Then he added, his tone uncertain, "You will keep it, Maeve?"

She looked up at him. The slightest of frowns drew his eyebrows together over those dark, unreadable eyes. She wanted to smooth away that line. Instead she nodded, unable to give words to her agreement to this folly of meeting him like this, as if her lack of words somehow made it seem more of an accidental thing, not a planned and much desired tryst.

"Good. Until then." He hesitated, and then with a stiff flourish he kissed her hand. "You see, already I start to gain fine manners. Sleep well, Maeve."

It took her a moment to realize that she was still standing next to him, staring at him, so near she could smell the spice in his scent. She recovered her wits and fled, her heart pounding as fast as her feet.

When she got to her room, she shut the door behind her and leaned against it, her eyes pressed shut and madness in her heart.

You are a fool, the voice whispered in her head.

How was she ever to go on with this position? And how was she ever to contain her impatience for Thursday?

Andrew greeted Maeve the following morning with what he thought sounded a proper lordly tone. He had seen the flush on her face last night when they had parted.

He had felt the slight tremble in her small hand when he had taken it and kissed it. He had frightened her with that ridiculous gesture.

It had been a silly impulse. A boy's desire to impress. He had acted without thinking, and had been well served for his impudence by her instant flight away from him.

Damn, what must she have thought?

Well, that would not happen again. His days of being an impetuous hothead were well past. Today, he would reassure her. He would treat her as what she was—a valuable employee. He wanted her to know that he had no intention of abusing his power over her, for he was aware, in a way he had not been before, of just how precarious her position was at Rothe House.

She was not a servant, but she worked here for her keep. She was a lady, but she had lost the rights of such a state. The other servants gave her a certain deferential treatment, due in part to his own orders, and due to her innate dignity. Yet she had no authority over them. She was, in short, very like a prisoner of war. Only her prison was an invisible one, marked by the invisible bars between the world of privilege and the world of servitude.

He did not like to think that he had put her in a difficult situation by acting anything but a gentleman. After all, he did not want her to quit. He wanted her happy. He wanted her to stay.

As for his reasons for this desire, he had already established those in his mind this morning as he shaved and dressed. Clarissa needed someone to look after her. And Maeve was good with Dorothy. He had also finally admitted to himself, as he allowed his fussy valet to tie his cravat, that he enjoyed Maeve's company—God, how good it had felt to hear her say his name.

However, he liked the company of any number of persons—his steward, for one. Or Edward Laurence, whom he had recently hired as a secretary. Yes, he liked quite a few people, and he also enjoyed having Maeve around.

He saw no need to look deeper for a reason for his feelings, for he had gotten out of the habit of doing so, and what did not exist inside him could not hurt him.

So he turned his thoughts intentionally away from any introspection and focused his attention on Maeve.

"I trust you slept well," he said, sitting down again as she took her chair at the breakfast table.

The room lay on the south side of the house, and normally its yellow walls and tall windows gave it a sunny aspect. Today, however, Maeve's skin looked pale against the yellow, and she seemed a tiny thing in her tight, faded brown dress.

She ducked her chin shyly. "Yes. Thank you, my lord."

He nodded and returned to reading his paper. Rather, he stared at the print, and thought that she did not eat enough. His fierce terrier needed more than a buttered slice of toast and a few sips of coffee to keep her in fighting fitness.

It was the food, he decided.

When he had returned home, he had left the household management to Dorothy. But she had turned melodramatic and declared it was his house and his staff to order as he pleased. He refused to do so, meaning that the house was like an unwound clock that was slowly coming to a standstill.

Well, he would have to take matters in hand and see if Mrs. Henderson could convince Cook to serve more appetizing meals. Perhaps if Maeve put on enough weight, she would split the seams on that awful brown dress and be forced into more suitable garments.

Thoughts of how he would rather see Maeve dressed vanished when Clarissa arrived, in chattering spirits.

Andrew rose, greeted his niece and started to excuse

himself. A disapproving glance from Maeve stopped him. Chastened, he sat down again.

Maeve frowned again when he started to bury himself in his paper. He glanced at her, caught the subtle request in her eyes, and wished he'd had as potent a weapon, during the Peninsular campaign, as a pair of speaking gray eyes.

Setting aside *The London Times*—a periodical for which he paid far too much to have it posted to him for him to ignore—he asked Clarissa, "So, miss, what do you plan to do today?"

Clarissa glanced at him, startled, then eyed him with deep suspicion. "I haven't done anything."

"Yes, but what do you plan to do? You must have some plans?"

After casting a worried look at Maeve, Clarissa reluctantly and slowly began to talk about her day. Andrew listened, realizing that he must be the biggest idiot in history never to have thought to ask his niece such a simple question. She rattled on about plans to sketch with Miss Midden in the garden, to visit with Lady Rothe that afternoon, and then to take the steward's daughters out for an al fresco tea. What he heard, however, was the yearning of a lonely girl.

"Why do you not have friends over?" he demanded suddenly.

Clarissa bit her lower lip and glanced at Maeve. "I . . . I . . ."

"Don't you know anyone?" he asked, frowning.

Maeve answered. "I believe, sir, that the neighbors await your calls before they will pay a visit here. Mrs. Henderson says they're waiting for a sign that the household is officially out of mourning for your brother."

"But it's been nearly nine . . . oh, very well." He gave a sigh and rose. "I see I shall have to make more adjustments to my schedule."

Clarissa sat up, her eyes gleaming. "Oh, would you, sir? Oh, that would be lovely. And I would be happy to come with you on visits."

"We shall see," he answered, and left without risking a glance at Maeve's face, for he could feel her stare on him and he knew that if he met that approving glance of hers he would probably be led into promising even more.

In his study, he found Edward Laurence, his secretary, waiting for him, a list already in hand for the building materials that needed to be purchased to start the work to restore the ruined wing.

Andrew went over the list—the limestone to be sent over from Lord Elgin's quarry, the timber for beams, the new windows and fittings to come from London. All of it somehow irritated him. He had set out to restore the ruined wing, so why should that task now seem less pleasing? It would be lovely when it was done—but would Maeve still meet him there? Or perhaps she would be gone by then—off to some new position.

He looked up and saw his earnest young secretary staring at him, and he realized suddenly that Edward had asked him a question.

"Yes, yes, whatever you see fit," he answered, handing back the list to Edward.

The young man brightened. He was plain and thin and had the somber temperament one would expect from the eldest son of a vicar. "Then you do not mind if I journey to Bath to inquire about the possibility of using stone from my uncle's house? He means to tear down a wing, and it seems a shame to allow the stone not to be put to use elsewhere. However, the transportation costs—"

"Bath?" Andrew said, sitting back in his chair. "You've an uncle there?"

"Yes, my lord. My mother's brother."

Andrew rested his elbows on his chair arms and steepled his fingers. Maeve's references had included that she had run a school for girls just outside of Bath. She had seemed uncomfortable when he had asked about her past last night, and he had curbed his curiosity. But still the desire to know more about her nagged at him. A few inquiries would not be out of place—and he might find some clue as to what had left her so skittish about society. After all, if he could banish that fear for her, perhaps she would stay. But, he told himself, he only wanted Maeve to stay so that she might escort Clarissa into society, of course.

"Yes. Why didn't I think of that before?" he muttered.

Edward adjusted his gold wire spectacles. "Perhaps because you did not know my uncle had a house there?"

"What? Oh, the house. Yes, I think you ought to go to Bath at once to ask your uncle about purchasing that stone. Before you return, however, I want you to stay in the district a week or so and make another set of inquiries: these about Miss Midden's Academy for Girls."

Twelve

"It's here!" Clarissa said, bursting into Maeve's room like a too bright summer's morn. The girl bounded across the room with unladylike strides, her golden hair streaming loose behind her. She had on a white muslin day dress, but she looked as if she had scrambled into it, for the blue ribbons at the high waist were untied and the back was barely laced.

At the tall windows which overlooked the front of the house, Clarissa threw back the dark blue velvet curtains. "Oh, do come and see! There is the largest wagon in the drive and they are trying to figure out how to unload the crate without smashing anyone or anything."

With a smothered yawn, Maeve sat up, her eyes bleary, her brain sleep-fogged. "My dear child, what hour is it?" She squinted across the room to the clock on the mantel, and gave a groan. "Clarissa, it's not even six in the morning!"

"Oh, never mind that." Clarissa skipped across to Maeve's bed and pulled away the covers. "This is the most excitement we've had here in months. You must come," she insisted, like a child at Christmas. "Please. It's my grand piano."

Struggling not to yawn again, Maeve allowed the girl to drag her to the window. She had never liked mornings and she had to clamp down now upon the uncivil urge to send Clarissa away with a sharp command so that she could crawl back into the warm clutches of her bed.

Clarissa let go of Maeve's arm and threw open the window sash. Cold air slapped Maeve's face, making her blink and awaken. Across from the house, mist clung to the lush grass of the home farm pastures and dark brown cows stood, flicking their tails and chewing their grass and watching the house.

Shouts drew Maeve's attention to the scene below.

On the graveled front drive, a wagon and team waited patiently, with a large crate in the flat wagon bed. One man stood beside the heads of the heavy draft horses, keeping them still, while another walked around the wagon, undoing the ropes that tied the crate in place. Servants popped in and out of the house, throwing open the double-wide front doors, bumping into each other and scurrying to obey Lord Rothe's commands.

He stood at the top of the steps dressed in boots, breeches and a chocolate brown riding coat, as if he had been up and about for hours already. He was hatless, and the morning breeze ruffled his dark hair. He seemed the one calm soul in the flurry of activity, and Maeve had the distinct impression from his relaxed stance and unflustered tone that he was enjoying himself.

Clarissa leaned her elbows on the windowsill. "Isn't it the biggest wagon you have ever seen? Uncle Andrew sent a footman to get the four biggest stable hands just to help unload it."

Maeve leaned out as well for a better view. Just as she did, Lord Rothe's voice carried up to her. "No, no, we won't need block and tackle. It's a ramp we want, and poles to roll the crate upon."

Next to Maeve, Clarissa giggled. "He sounds as if he's moving a cannon, not my piano."

Maeve smiled. "I don't believe there is anything that

puts Lord Rothe into better spirits than to have everyone jumping to his orders."

"Well, he does it very well. I must admit, he's rather handsome when he's like this, isn't he? I'd always thought him old, for he's always glowering at me, but he looks . . . well, he looks rather dashing right now, don't you think so?"

Maeve did think so.

His lordship had taken one step down, so that he stood with one booted foot upon the top stair. He had one hand upon his hip, and an air of command radiated from him. Maeve propped her chin on her hand and let herself enjoy the spectacle below.

The burly stable hands with their sleeves rolled up and their muscles gleaming made a stirring sight, but Maeve's stare kept slipping to the man on the stairs who stood out in his dark coat. How unfair it was that he should have a better pair of shoulders than any other man present. Why was it that he drew the eye when there were so many others milling around?

"Hallo, Uncle," Clarissa called out, and waved.

Maeve froze in place, mortified.

Andrew glanced up, his eyes narrowed and searching. He saw the sun glint off Clarissa's hair; then he saw Maeve and he forgot about his niece.

Maeve had been leaning her chin upon her hand, but now she straightened. She wore something thin and white that clung to her curves, and her thick braid hung down over one shoulder in a tousled dark rope. She must have just risen from her bed, for he caught a glimpse of her face, deliciously sleepy, her cheeks rosy.

Then she disappeared.

She must have dragged Clarissa away from the window as well, for he could see no one now.

He knew he ought to be angry with Clarissa for leaning out the window to "halloo" as if she were a tavern wench, not a young lady of the house. But he could not get his mind past the image of Maeve in her nightclothes.

He looked up again, hoping for one more glance of her, then turned back to the task at hand, bemused, distracted, somewhat disturbed by his own reaction and already pushing it aside as something he did not want to think about.

Maeve pulled herself and Clarissa back inside the room, her cheeks burning. "Clarissa, young ladies do not hang out windows to call down to their uncles."

Clarissa dropped her chin, but the look in her eyes did not remain penitent for very long. "You're right, Miss Midden. So let us go downstairs and watch."

She started to tug Maeve to the door, but Maeve stood firm. "Not with me in my nightclothes. And not with your hair dangling down, or those tradesmen will mistake you for a child of twelve."

"Oh, you don't think they could?" Clarissa asked, horrified by the thought.

"Let us hope they do, for that is the only excuse for your behavior. Now, go let your maid make you presentable, and we shall both be down soon enough that we shall not miss anything."

In the end, they missed the lowering of the piano off the wagon. But they were downstairs in time to see the servants haul the crate up the ramp Lord Rothe had ordered improvised upon the front steps.

Maeve tried to keep Clarissa out from underfoot, and tried to keep herself very much out of Lord Rothe's line of sight. She did such a good job of this that he did not seem to notice them at all. Perversely, Maeve found this worse than having been seen in her nightdress.

When the crate had been conveyed to the back of the house and into the music room, Maeve glanced at Clarissa, who had fallen silent. Her stare was distant, and

the faintest wetness glistened across her blue eyes like a
mist over a lake.

"What is it?" Maeve asked, unable to guess what had
caused this sudden dampening of the girl's high spirits.

Clarissa at once put on an over-bright smile that did
nothing to light up her eyes. "Oh, it's nothing. Isn't it
amazing how they can put a grand piano in that flat a
box? I suppose they will attach the legs once it is out—
but how will they do that? Will they have to turn it upside
down, do you suppose?"

Maeve shook her head. "Am I such a poor friend that
you try to put me off with so weak a story?"

The girl tried to hold her smile, but it slowly faded and
sorrow clouded her eyes again. "It's just foolishness,
that's all. For a moment I . . . well, I wished that Mama
or Papa were here to share this. But that is just child-
ishness, I know, and I am quite grown up now, so it does
not matter." She smiled again and began to chatter, but
her eyes did not brighten and Maeve was not fooled.

Clarissa moved aside to watch as Lord Rothe began to
give orders for the uncrating of the piano.

The music room sat at the back of the house on the
first floor. One wall of casement windows opened out
onto the formal rose garden, and behind the soft, fragrant
colors the towering cliffs of the Gordale Scar stood in
sharp contrast. On the wall opposite the windows hung
paintings of classical scenes done in the style of Rubens.
The room lay nearly bare, except for an unused harp in
the far corner. No carpets covered the parquet floor to
muffle the sound, so the room with all those in it now
seemed noisy and busy.

Maeve watched for a moment, her thoughts troubled.
The sight of Clarissa standing by herself undid all of her
resolve to stop meddling. It would not be meddling, after
all, simply to ask Lady Rothe if she would care to come
downstairs.

Maeve had no problem slipping away unnoticed.

She started down the hall toward the main stairs, rehearsing various speeches as she went, but these died when she reached the base of the stairs and looked up.

On the upper landing, Lady Rothe stood, one hand tight upon the banister, her eyes glazed over and her face ashen.

Maeve started to smile; then she hesitated. The unnatural stillness, the blank look in her ladyship's eyes—something was dreadfully wrong. An alarm began to pulse through her.

"My lady?" Maeve said, lifting her skirts to hurry up the stairs. Out of breath, she reached Lady Rothe's side and put a hand out to touch her arm. It was like touching ice.

She put a gentle arm around Lady Rothe. "Please come back to your room. You should not have gotten up. You are not well."

It took a moment more of coaxing, of tugging to loosen Lady Rothe's clawlike grip upon the banister, before Maeve could lead the woman back to her room. All the time, Lady Rothe stared straight in front of her, unseeing, her breath shallow and alarmingly rapid.

Worry twisted in Maeve's stomach, along with guilt for ever having thought that Lady Rothe might be feigning her ailments as a means to attract attention.

When she had Lady Rothe back in her room and seated on a satin-covered daybed, Maeve started away, saying, "I'll just call Lord Rothe to—"

"No!" Lady Rothe said, sitting up so quickly that Maeve swung around, startled. Lady Rothe grabbed Maeve's arm. "Not Andrew. You must not tell him. He hates me so much already. He would only think me weak, and I am . . ."

Her voice trailed off as she buried her face in her plump, quivering hands.

Maeve returned to her side at once and laid a tentative hand on her arm. "My lady, you do him an injustice. But, if you prefer, I will stay with you."

Whatever spell had held Lady Rothe frozen seemed to have broken. She let go of Maeve to fumble around her for a handkerchief. Maeve went to her ladyship's dresser, found a lacy confection scented with lavender and brought it back.

Lady Rothe dabbed at her eyes, then she clutched at Maeve's arm again, drawing her closer so that she must sit down on the daybed. "You are such a dear. You think everyone has as much feeling as you, but, you must trust me, I know my brother-in-law. I once nearly married the man."

"So I have heard," Maeve said, shifting uncomfortably so that the satin squeaked underneath her.

Her ladyship went on, her voice pitched too high and her words tumbling out too fast for Maeve to do anything but worry at this babbling flow.

"I was weak even then. I let him convince me that I loved him. Of course, I was not much older than Clarissa, and his music . . . oh, I adored how passionately he played his music. But I should never have promised him anything. He hated me when I told him I would not follow the drum, and I would not wait for his return. How could he have ever expected me to wait, after all? I did not know if it would be one year, or five years, or ten. And he put it all on my shoulders by saying I was all he had left! As if that were true! He was always so cruel to me! Phillip never was."

Lady Rothe buried her face again, this time in the tiny square of lace handkerchief.

A lump lodged in Maeve's throat. She knew how easy it was for a girl to make a hero out of an ordinary man. But her sympathy lay more with the man who had been rejected so many years ago. She could not help thinking of how she had seen him that night of the storm after a man had died. He was a man who felt things deeply. How very much it must have damaged him to first lose his music and then to lose the woman he loved.

However, her pain for what had happened to others long ago did nothing to remedy the moment. Maeve pushed away her dark thoughts and her feelings and took up Lady Rothe's hand.

"Perhaps he was not what you thought him, but he is far from uncaring now. Nor does he hold the past against you. He is a gentleman, and I cannot believe he would be unkind to you."

Lady Rothe shook her head. "But he is. You don't know. You weren't here when he came home. It's not what he does . . . it's what he does not do. He acts from duty only . . . his duty, his honor . . . oh, I hate those things. He does not act from feeling. He never has. Phillip never spoke to me of duty and obligation. Phillip was a real gentleman. He came to me when he heard that Andrew was leaving, and he told me how he felt, and, oh, he was all Andrew could not be. He always told me how much he loved me. Not like Andrew. Andrew has no heart!"

Maeve pressed her lips tight together. She had an irrational urge to slap her ladyship for this near-hysterical nonsense. However, that would not do. So she took on the tone she would use with a difficult pupil.

"Very well, my lady, if you insist."

"Dorothy . . . you must call me Dorothy," her ladyship said, pouting and sniffling like a child half Clarissa's age.

"Dorothy, I will not tell Lord Rothe what happened, but you must let me get you some help. You looked as if you had had a seizure on the stairway. What if you had fallen?"

The color fled Dorothy's face, leaving her pasty. Her eyes seemed sunken and her face aged in an instant. "Oh,

God. Not that. Not again," she said, her voice a whisper, her lower lip starting to tremble.

"Again? You fell down the stairs before?"

Dorothy nodded. "He . . . we . . . that night . . . that last night . . . we were coming home from dinner at the Faradays. They set a dreadful table, but Phillip never could refuse anyone's invitation. He joked all the way home about Mrs. Faraday's miserly ideas of entertainment. We were just coming up the stairs together. He was a step behind me. We paused and . . ."

She broke off and swallowed hard. Her blue eyes glazed over, her face crumpled. "He said his arm hurt. That's the last thing he said to me. 'My dear, my arm hurts.' I turned, and he looked at me with such an awful look. It frightened me. I'd never seen such anguish on his face. So I took his hand. And then he . . . he clutched at his chest with his other hand. I was so frightened. I called out to him . . . and then suddenly we both seemed to be falling . . ."

A whimper escaped her, and she covered her face, her shoulders shaking and her body racked by the most wrenching sobs.

Maeve took the other woman in her arms and rocked her as she would a fretful infant. "It's over. It must have been like a nightmare, but it is over now."

They sat so for a moment, with Maeve's arms around Lady Rothe. When the sobs lessened, Maeve released her hold.

Dorothy sat up and dabbed at her face. "I do not know who or how the servants got me to my bed. And then I could not leave it for weeks, for I had broken a rib and my ankle. The doctor came and gave me awful medicine to drink."

She stopped and seemed to shrink in on herself. Her tears flowed unchecked, carving deep grooves in the powder on her face. "Maeve, I never saw him again. A lady is not supposed to go to a funeral. And I could not have, even had I been allowed, because I could not walk. Sometimes at night I slip from my room now and go to his portrait, and I just sit with him and wish that I could have seen him one last time."

Helpless longing washed over Maeve. Nothing she could say would ease this loss. Some things could not be mended—not by words, or by time. She wanted to cry for this poor woman. She realized that she had felt envy for Lady Rothe, for her position and her family. Now she looked at her and simply saw a woman torn by guilt, by loss, by fear. So she sat with her and hoped that companionship would at least help these difficult memories fade away again.

"Thank you for telling me this," Maeve said when Lady Rothe's tears began to dry. "But, do you know, I doubt that your husband would have wanted you to see him again. I think part of that anguish you saw in his eyes was because he knew he was leaving you, and he was upset by it. Men do hate us to think them vain, but they hate it even worse for us to glimpse them at anything but their best. Think how much he would have hated your seeing him with him being anything but a splendid fellow.

"And you have Clarissa. You must always remember that. You have only to look at her to see your husband, for Lord Rothe says he sees his brother in her all the time."

Dorothy's lower lip began to tremble. "But I don't have her. I'm losing her. I tried to come down today. To be with her. I heard her taking you downstairs to see her piano—she sounded so excited. I wanted so badly to be with her. Only I cannot. I cannot." She looked around her suddenly, her eyes flashing and her voice thick. "I hate this room. I hate it! It's become my prison!"

She started to cry again, a keen wailing. Desperation began to eat away at Maeve's sympathy. This could not go on. Lady Rothe would drive herself into an early grave, and then Clarissa would be that orphan of the melodrama she had invented. That would not happen, Maeve promised herself.

"My lady . . . Dorothy," Maeve said, taking Lady Rothe's shoulders and turning her so that she had to look straight into Maeve's eyes. "You sound as if you would do anything to be able to share your daughter's life again."

Dorothy nodded, her blue eyes faded but enormous in her puffy, reddened face. "Anything . . . anything but those stairs. I cannot face them. Every time I stand there, I see Philip, I—"

"If I find a way to get you down them, a way that means you have to do nothing but close your eyes, will you do so?" Maeve asked, her tone harsh. This was no time for sympathetic words.

Dorothy sniffled like a child and then nodded.

"Good. Then this is what you must do," Maeve said, and she began to lay out her plan.

Lord Rothe glanced around, pleased at how well the work was going and wanting to see Maeve's reaction. It had been her idea, after all, to take Clarissa to York, so she was the indirect instigator of this piano. He wanted to see the approval shining in her eyes, turning the gray to nearly blue. He wanted to see her face turned up to his, delight glowing on her skin. He wanted to preen just a little for how well he had managed it all. Instead, he could not find her trim figure clad in that awful brown dress.

Clarissa stood nearby, shooting coy glances at the stable hands.

But no Maeve.

Irritated, he strode into the hall and immediately heard

her voice coming from the main stairs. "Oh, do be careful, Seth. No, don't look just yet."

Curiosity mixed with irritation, stirring into a volatile combination that set his temper on edge. Seth, he knew damn well, was one of the grooms, but what the devil was the man doing with Maeve?

He strode to the front of the house, his jaw tight, his fists clenching. He stopped near the foot of the stairs, brought up short by the startling parade descending the stairs.

Seth led the small group, his hulking six-foot form dwarfing even the grandeur of the main stairway. Slung over Seth's broad shoulder like an unwieldy, white muslin-clad sack of grain, Andrew saw the unmistakable shape of a woman.

Good God—Dorothy, Andrew thought, his mouth falling open.

Small, nervous squeaks emitted from Lady Rothe, but since she was hung over Seth's shoulder in that undignified fashion—tiny feet and large rump first—Andrew could not see her expression.

Behind this unlikely duo, Maeve followed, her face as calm as ever, her concentration totally on Lady Rothe, as she said, "No, not yet. Don't look yet. You promised."

"What the deuce is this—a game?" Andrew demanded, folding his arms to wait for the ungainly trio to finish their descent. Maeve scowled at him, and he thought that she had no reason to be so irritated with him. It was his house. He had a right to know what the devil was going on in it.

Dorothy squeaked again. Seth glanced up and gave his usual half-witted, gap-toothed grin before coming down the last few steps.

Arriving on solid ground, Seth set his burden on her feet and pulled off his cap, glancing around him like an eager child awaiting praise. He was not the brightest of grooms, but he was good with horses. And carrying ladies down stairs as well, it seemed.

Andrew turned to his sister-in-law for an explanation.

Dorothy let out a nervous giggle, smoothed her tousled hair, glanced up the stairs and started to faint.

"Oh, the devil," Andrew swore, reaching for her at the same time Seth did. Dorothy fell into their arms, a dead—and hefty—weight.

Andrew winced under the burden and told the groom, "Since you've such a talent for it, you may take her ladyship into the front drawing room, Seth. Then send for the doctor."

"Oh, there's no need for a doctor," Maeve said.

Andrew glanced at her, then turned back to the groom. "Very well. No doctor. But see that Lady Rothe is settled on a couch in the front drawing room."

Seth nodded his comprehension, offered up another grin and then lumbered away with his burden.

Andrew turned to Maeve. "Now, what is all this? Why is Seth hauling Dorothy around in that fashion? If she doesn't need a doctor, then what the devil is wrong with her, and why are you now avoiding my gaze?"

Maeve pulled back her shoulders and finally looked up to meet his stare. "I beg your pardon, my lord. I am not at liberty to explain everything, but suffice it to say, Seth was helping her ladyship down the stairs."

She looked upset. Her face had lost its color, and she held her mouth pressed tight, flattening out the soft curves of her lips. He suddenly wanted to touch his thumb to those lips, until they smoothed and parted and smiled and . . .

He pulled his thoughts back to the matter at hand, and clasped his hands behind his back. "That was not helping. That was hauling. If she's that ill, she ought to stay in her bed. What possessed you to allow her to—"

"She did not allow it. I did," Lady Rothe said, on her

feet and standing in the hall. Her gown and hair still looked as if she had dressed in the dark, both hanging slightly askew, but she stood with her back as straight as it had been when she was a girl, and with all the regal command of a titled lady.

Andrew let his stare rake over her, impatience with her simmering in his blood. Those impossibly large blue eyes of hers were the only resemblance she bore to the girl he'd once loved to distraction. Her figure had thickened beyond recognition. Red splotches marred her complexion, but that could have come from being hung upside down. He had forgotten how slight of stature she was—she barely came up to his chin—but she stared up at him now as cold and disdainful as ever.

He gave her a small, ironic bow and said, his tone dry, "It seems you are not at your deathbed after all. How nice of you to finally recover."

Both her chins came up. "I never said I was dying. But I am much recovered, thank you."

He frowned at her. "Dorothy, you've been in your bed for the better part of a year, claiming one illness and then another, all of which baffled every doctor in the county. How is it that you are now well enough to come downstairs? Are you done playing the grieving widow? And why is it that you come down in that fashion, slung over a groom's shoulder? Good God, no wonder Clarissa acts a hoyden, when her mother shows no better conduct!"

Dorothy's eyes glistened with tears. She turned to Maeve. "You see? Just as I said." She fixed Andrew with a cold stare. "Heartless!"

Maeve saw Lord Rothe's mouth tighten and she knew a bloody war of words was about to begin. She stepped between the potential combatants before another volley could be launched. "My lord, we very much required Seth's aid. You see, Lady Rothe's condition does not allow her to deal with stairs. It is that which has kept her to her rooms, but she has decided to make her bedchamber on the first floor here so that she can more easily fit back into her old life."

"Stairs? What the devil's wrong with you that you can't go up and down a flight of stairs?"

For a moment, the hall was silent. Lord Rothe locked stares with his sister-in-law. The pulse beat in his jaw in a dangerous tempo, and Dorothy's lower lip quivered with the warning of impending hysterics.

Maeve took a deep breath and committed herself to a very small lie. "It is a weakness in her ankle. Left over from when it was broken last year."

His lordship turned to her, one dark eyebrow raised in a skeptical quirk. She met his stare, trying to implore him to accept this answer as an alternative to Dorothy's tears.

"Odd the doctors never mentioned such a weakness to me," he said, his tone skeptical.

The weight of his stare nearly undid Maeve's resolve to try and help Dorothy keep her fears secret. A hot blush stained her cheeks. *Oh, please do not ask anything more*, she implored in a silent glance sent at him. *I cannot tell it to you now.*

He met that glance, his dark eyes still glittering, but she saw his mouth soften ever so slightly. One dark eyebrow rose, and then he turned to Dorothy. "And what room will you want for your bedchamber? My study, perhaps? The library?"

"Good heavens, no," Dorothy said, pulling her dignity together, despite that she was dressed in an untidy confection of lawn and muslin and ribbons. "Maeve and I decided I should take the small parlor in the southeast wing, next to the breakfast room. I used to adore sewing in it. You may have my things brought down today, though I expect the room will need to be done over with new drapery and fittings, but that will be for later. Now, you must excuse me. I want to see my daughter's new grand piano."

She swept away from them without so much as a limp to her step. Maeve watched Lord Rothe's expression, noting the skeptical eyebrow rise a notch higher, but at least a glimmer of amusement now lurked in his eyes.

He turned to face her. "I do hope you know what you are about with this."

"Whatever do you mean?" she asked.

Andrew studied her open face, her clear gray eyes that now carried a touch of defiant blue in their depths, her stubborn chin. She would always be one to think of others before herself. Only he very much worried that she had put them both in a spot which they would one day regret.

"Did you ever stop to think," he said, "that with Dorothy an invalid, you could have stayed here as her companion long after Clarissa married?"

She blinked up at him, her eyes enormous in her face, her expression smoothing into one of utter surprise.

He had to smile at that. She looked adorably confused. "No, you did not think, did you? You simply saw a need and stepped in to see it filled. You are a godsend for us, Miss Midden. I wish we deserved you."

She glanced down, and her tiny hands fluttered over her ghastly dress, smoothing it. A sweep of rosy hue swept over her cheeks in a way that made him want to lift her chin so that he could look into her eyes.

"I . . . I believe Lady Rothe will need me," she said, her voice flustered. She turned and hurried away.

Lord Rothe remained standing in the hall, a distracted frown reclaiming his expression. He tried to ignore the worry that had started deep in him and which slowly grew until it sang along his nerves and vibrated in him like a discordant chord. He knew the signs of a battle turning

against him, and he feared he saw them now. For if
Dorothy took over Clarissa's supervision, what excuse
would he have to hold on to Maeve?

Thirteen

The letter arrived two weeks later, both too soon and too late, Maeve thought, staring miserably at Mr. Jessup's hastily penned lines.

She had come down early to breakfast, for Lady Rothe had expressed her desire to visit the Faradays today, taking with her Clarissa and Maeve. Before that ordeal, Maeve had wanted a few moments to herself.

Freeing Lady Rothe from her rooms had much the same double-edged effect as releasing a jinni from its bottle. Lady Rothe had certainly fulfilled many of Clarissa's wishes, but with the good came the bad. Her ladyship had set the household on its ear with the relocation and redecoration of her rooms, and she spurred the staff into a flurry of activity, setting Cook to learning new recipes and sending out invitations for small affairs. Lady Rothe acted not at all like a woman who had been until a short time ago a sickly invalid.

She even started taking Clarissa on visits to see the neighbors. Which meant Maeve was obliged to accompany them. No one intentionally snubbed her at these gatherings, but Maeve felt the difficulty of being an outsider. She sat silent and isolated, forced apart both by her status as a companion and by the simple fact that she could not laugh and reminisce with these people. She tried to fade into the background, and she succeeded well enough that everyone seemed to forget her.

It was a good reminder to her that she was an employee, not a guest, at Rothe House.

She had forgotten that. And somehow she managed to forget it again on those nights when she had her rendezvous with the colonel . . . with Lord Rothe. That pattern of meeting him, laughing with him, talking to him, had woven a dangerous contentment. Maeve had given herself totally to the enjoyment of his company while she had it.

Now, staring at the letter from Mr. Jessup, she realized the price she must pay for that indulgence. She had only made it harder on herself to leave now that Mr. Jessup had found her a new post. The ideal post. She must make a choice—and make it soon.

Clarissa came in to breakfast, smiling and happy. Maeve folded Mr. Jessup's letter and pocketed it, greeting the girl as if nothing were amiss. There would be time later, when she had made up her mind, to tell the others. A few moments later Lord Rothe joined them. Lady Rothe still took her chocolate and toast in bed, the one invalid habit that she had not shed.

Clarissa filled up the conversation with news and gossip and stories, but Maeve was aware of Lord Rothe's inquiring stare upon her, as if he had sensed her troubled thoughts. She also felt Mr. Jessup's letter crinkle in her pocket.

Oh, why had he not written sooner? Or never at all?

"Are you feeling well, Miss Midden?"

Maeve glanced up to meet Lord Rothe's dark eyes. He was frowning at her, the small vertical line pulling his eyebrows together.

She gave a perfunctory smile. "I am just a little tired. Who did you say would be coming to dinner next week, Clarissa?"

Clarissa launched into an exhaustive description of the guest list for a small dinner—not more than ten couples—to assemble at Rothe House next week.

Maeve kept her attention fixed on Clarissa, though she continued to feel his lordship's frown upon her.

Finally he rose and excused himself to attend to the business of the day. Maeve closed her eyes for a moment and wished she had the luxury of commanding her own time. However, she reminded herself sternly that she was well paid to be at someone's beck and call, so when Lady Rothe sent for her, she put on her bonnet and went to call upon people she did not know.

The day dragged on forever, filled with too little activity to forget Mr. Jessup's letter and too much to allow Maeve to pull it out again. It was not until they returned to Rothe House and it was time to dress for dinner that Maeve was able to retreat to her room. There, she dragged off her bonnet with a sigh of relief, and then settled in the window seat to pull out Mr. Jessup's letter and read it again.

Dear Miss Midden,

I have found for you the perfect position with a family situated just outside Bath. Mr. Bridges made his fortune in Bristol trade, and now wishes a genteel upbringing for his six girls. You need not fear that the family has social pretensions. They merely wish to offer their girls every advantage, but do not care to subject them to the possible indignities of a boarding school. When I mentioned your qualities, Mrs. Bridges expressed a keen desire to meet you at once. Please give me the favor of a reply as to the earliest date when you might meet with the Bridges, for they wish to fill this position at once.

Yr. Servant,
Wilm. Jessup

Six girls. Was that not exactly what she had told Mr. Jessup she had wanted? A family who did not even wish

to launch their daughters into the society that so filled
Maeve with apprehension. No more moving from house
to house. No more uncertainty for her future.

No more midnight meetings in a ruined wing.

Maeve stared out the window of her room, her feelings
at war with her thoughts. This was what she had dreamed
of—so why could she not be happy about it?

The days had grown longer, and the softness of the
fading light cast the world into rosy hues. Across the
green lawn, Lord Rothe strode toward the house, two
dogs frolicking around his heels. Spaniels, she guessed
from their flopping ears and brown and white markings.
Not the lapdog size kept by Lady Rothe, but bounding,
boisterous, sporting dogs that suited his lordship's long
stride.

He paused, picked up a stick and threw it. The dogs
tore off in tandem after the prize.

Maeve put a hand up to the window and spread her
fingers over the cold glass.

How could she leave?

How could she ever stay?

She turned away from the view outside, disgusted with
herself for her weakness. She had acted before with her
heart, making a decision that had led to nothing but
shame and anguish. She had sworn never to be so foolish
or rash again, yet here she was, allowing her feelings to
rule her, rather than taking the obvious and sensible
course of action.

Quickly she dressed for dinner, changing from her
brown dress to her black one, draping over her arms the
lovely fringed shawl that Lady Rothe had given her. Then
she sat at the small writing table in her room to make up
two lists—one the advantages in staying at Rothe House,
and one the benefits in this new position.

She redid her lists three times, unsatisfied each time

with the results. But no matter how she tried, the logical conclusion came out the same.

It was time to go.

"Isn't it biblical women who go about braiding their hair before they start some trouble?" Andrew spoke lightly, his voice pitched low and faintly amused.

Maeve had arrived before him this evening. She sat on the stone floor, a single candle beside her, braiding her hair. Or perhaps she had been unbraiding it. He could not tell, for half of it lay in a neat plait that fell over her shoulder and the bottom half curled wildly about, dark and tempting. His fingers twitched at the thought of bunching its softness in his hands.

"I wish you would let it hang loose. Just this once," he said, speaking his thoughts. "You look too much the governess when it is so tightly done up."

He carried a rolled carpet under one arm and a branch of candles in the other hand. He came into the room, spread the carpet and then helped her to a seat on it.

She hesitated a moment, the color high in her cheeks, and then she pulled loose the half-done braid. Her hair curled in dark tendrils, softening her round face and giving a startling contrast to her white skin.

"And the nightcap?" he asked, daring more now that she had obliged him in one matter. "It's terribly fetching—for a grandmother."

She kept her stare lowered, but she pulled off the white nightcap, and then bit her lower lip like a guilty schoolgirl.

He seated himself next to her, sitting cross-legged, Indian fashion. "Ah, much better. You know, I always thought your hair to be dark brown, like a seal's coat, but now I see there are gold threads woven there."

"And silver as well," she said, the faintest of smiles

pulling up her mouth. "I would not have you ignore them, for they come hard earned."

"Well, they flatter you," he said, settling the candles nearer so that they made the world seem no more than this intimate circle of light. "I expect I am to blame for a few of them . . . and so is Dorothy. Is she running you ragged? I shall have a word with her about that, if you like."

"No. Please don't. She is very kind to me, really."

"Then what has you looking so drawn? And don't tell me it is nothing. There's no spark to your eyes tonight, and you ate practically nothing at dinner. Did you think I would not notice?"

A telltale blush warmed her cheeks, but she met his stare with one as unblinking and open as his own. "You seemed occupied enough, dealing with Lady Rothe's desire to hold a birthday party for you."

He grimaced. "I don't know what put that particular bee in her bonnet, but I will be damned . . . beg pardon, I'll be dashed if I allow her to invite a dozen people I don't know to a dinner I would hate attending."

Maeve frowned. "Do you mind, my lord? I mean, what she's done."

"It's Andrew, remember. There is no rank between us here, and what should I mind?" He stretched out on the carpet, propping himself up on one elbow. His brocade evening waistcoat hung open over his shirt, and he had pulled off his cravat, leaving his shirt blessedly open at the neck. "Dorothy is only doing what she should have been doing. This was her house for nearly twenty years. I'd be the devil of a fellow to take its management away from her."

"You are very kind."

"And you give me too much credit. Dorothy's welcome to do what she likes, so long as she does not invade my study, argue with how I manage the estates, or spend herself into debt. But how is it that we are talking about her and me? My question for you still stands. Is she running you ragged?"

Maeve knew that the time had come to tell him. Yet, her throat tightened until she could not utter a word, and her heart seemed struck still in her chest. Her hand trembled as she reached into the pocket of her dressing gown and drew out Mr. Jessup's letter. She handed it to him.

"What's this?" he asked, sitting up. He scanned the note quickly, ran a hand through his hair, and then he stood up to pace away and back again.

Maeve sat very still, watching him. She had undone her hair for him because he had asked it of her. Would he ask more of her? And would she give it? Her hands trembled, so she hid them in her lap.

He scowled down at her and handed back the letter. "Will you take it, this . . . this perfect situation?"

She concentrated on folding the note again. "I . . . I have no reason to stay. My work here is done."

"Nonsense. Clarissa has come to depend upon you. And Dorothy is just as taken with you. Why can you not stay?" he demanded, his voice rough with an edge of anger.

"My lord . . . Andrew, will you be honest with me? When you hired me, was I not brought here as a wedge to dislodge Lady Rothe from her rooms? You do not need me now that her ladyship has taken on her duties."

His scowl darkened. "That is not to the point."

"That is exactly the point. I have no desire to go to London for Clarissa's debut, and you have no real need of me to do so. She has her mother now."

He strode away and then strode back. He had not worn his boots, and his stocking feet made no sound upon the stone floor. The dark scar of mountains outside the room loomed up, forever mute witnesses to the follies of humankind, their edges silvered by moonlight. Overhead, stars glittered indifferent to them, shining as brightly as they would over a pair of lovers. Misery welled up in Maeve, as large and dark as the mountains outside. They were going to part with an argument, and she did not want this as her last memory of their stolen time.

"What difference does it make that Dorothy is up and about?" he insisted. "She, as much as Clarissa, enjoys your company. Why, if it's work you need, stay on as her companion. My God, that could occupy you for years."

She looked down at her hands and forced them to remain still. "So I am to stay for Clarissa? And for Dorothy, Lady Rothe? For their sakes?"

"Well, yes. I hired you for that. And I'll match or better any salary. Besides, you're already settled here."

I hired you. The words echoed inside Maeve, falling like an iron weight into the emptiness where her heart should have been. She closed her eyes tightly. She had been so foolish to pretend that in this room it did not matter that he held the whip-hand in all their dealings.

I hired you.

She was his employee. Oh, he might enjoy her company, but he thought of her first as the companion he had hired for his niece. He had not forgotten that fact. He never would. He was well and truly a lord now.

She opened her eyes and took a deep breath. "Yes, you hired me. But my conditions of employment were that I would stay only until I found another position, or until you found my replacement. The former has come first. I have thought through the advantages and disadvantages— the chief of which is that Mr. Jessup sorely misrepresented this position to me before I arrived here, and that might be the case again. However, in reviewing all aspects, I am left with the same conclusion. I must think of my future, my lord. And a position with a large family of girls affords me more security than what we both know would be, at best, a stay here for a year or two."

There. She had gotten it out. She had not let one ounce of telltale emotion mar her voice. Underneath her dressing gown, she tugged her feet out of her slippers and dug her toes into the softness of the carpet. She wanted to cry, but she bit the inside of her cheek and refused to let her emotions rule her.

Andrew strode away and back again to loom over her. He did not understand her stubbornness in this matter. Damnation, what did she want of him? He did not understand her, and his anger mounted at how bloody unfair she was being about this whole bloody matter.

"Are you not treated well here? Is that why you wish to leave?" he demanded.

She did not look up to meet his stare, but answered, her voice tiny in the empty room, "I don't wish it. But as an employee, I must do many things I do not particularly wish to do, including moving on to positions where I shall be best employed. You are very kind—"

"Will you stop saying that!"

She jumped slightly, but she looked up and met his glower. Shadows hid half her face, but her eyes glittered with pride and defiance. "Please, do not yell. You may pay my salary, but that does not give you the right to raise your voice to me."

The sensation swept over him that he had stepped into a bog, for he could feel himself sinking. Panic rattled in his chest, but he could not let it out. God, how did he get back to solid ground?

The habits of battle took over. He frowned and shoved deeper his half-emerged fears and covered them over with simmering anger. She had started this with her pigheaded insistence and her damnable pride. She viewed her position here now as one of charity! My God, he should have worked her harder and then she would have no right to accuse him of "kindness."

He wanted to order her to stay. But she was not a sub-

altern he could command. *Damn it all.* He groped for
some other way to deal with the situation, but just as in
a bog, everything seemed to slip from his grasp. Her calm
voice and face, which had so attracted him at first, now
seemed a maddening irritation. He had to fold his hands
behind himself to keep from grabbing her and shaking
the sense into her head.

He took a pace away from her. Then, determined not
to shout at her again, his voice carefully controlled, he
said, "You seem to have thought this out thoroughly."

"A woman in my position must always consider her
actions carefully, for my choices are few, so I must make
the best of them."

"There is nothing I can say to change your mind? You
are set on leaving us?"

She looked up at him, and for an instant he swore that
he saw an unspoken plea shimmering in her eyes. It
passed like a shadow under a gray sea, and then vanished.
He could only believe that a trick of the candlelight had
put it there, for when she spoke, her voice was as calm
as always.

"If you will but view it rationally, my lord, you would
see I have no other choice."

He clenched his back teeth, and his stomach rolled with
anger. If she called him "my lord" once more in that prim
manner, he swore he would not be responsible for his
behavior. He raked his fingers through his hair again.

Something deep inside him clamored to get out. It tried
to push up past his fear and anger and growing helpless-
ness. He ignored it. The habit of years took over without
a thought, walling off and dismissing that stirring, desperate yearning. He could not act on the primitive urges
that fired his blood. She was in his hire. He was responsible for her. He could not drag her to him and compel
her to do as he asked by . . .

His mind slipped away from half-formed thoughts of

her in his arms, yielding to his kisses, giving way to him as he took possession of her.

Shocked by himself, he strode away, shaken to the core. Damnation, what was he thinking of? She was a lady, for God's sake. And he owed her the courtesy of treating her as such. When he came back, he had mastered himself, and could address her with as calm a voice as she had offered to him. "Will you allow me one favor?"

Maeve glanced up at Lord Rothe. Ice lay in his voice. The candles danced over his harsh features, making the flat planes of his cheeks gaunt and hollow. His black eyes glittered in the candlelight, hot as coals, and shadows darkened the hollows of his cheeks. Implacable lines framed the line of his mouth.

A shiver slipped through her. He looked more daunting than on that day they had first met.

He continued without waiting for her answer. "As you said before, Mr. Jessup can be somewhat . . . inaccurate in his descriptions of available situations. I would like you to make certain of this position before you leave my employ, so will you allow me to escort you to Bath?

"And if you say one more time that this is very kind of me, I shall be forced to demonstrate just how untrue that is. I act in my own interests. You are valuable to me. I do not wish to lose you as an employee here, but if I must do so, it will be to a situation that can offer you more."

The faint flare of hope that had blossomed in Maeve when he had first spoken of a favor wavered and died like a candle under a deluge. She had hoped that he would ask . . . well, for a more personal favor. A kiss, perhaps. Just one. A memory of his lips over hers, warm and demanding. She hung her head, ashamed for how desperately she wanted that physical touch from him, and how unable she was to ask for it, because, in all things, society dictated that a lady must wait to be asked.

She saw suddenly how the years would stretch out before her if she stayed. Her body would betray her again and again. She would start to hope. Her treacherous heart would start to imagine that he felt more for her than he did. She would spend her years weaving fantasies that had them together in this room, locked in each other's arms, passion laid as bare as their skins.

But it was only illusion.

He was a gentleman. A lord. He would never insult a woman with a kiss. Not unless he had courted her and she had accepted his suit . . . or unless he considered her unworthy of such consideration.

Self-pity began to swamp her. *Oh, why did I ruin my chances?* But she lifted her chin and fought it back. If she had never met Vincent, she would not be here now. And she would not have the wisdom to be wise and sensible.

She rose, ignoring the hand he held out to help her to her feet, using the excuse of the fall of her long hair over her face as a reason why she might not have seen the gesture. She could not trust herself to touch him. Her mind held only so much ability to enforce the calm exterior that covered the maelstrom of emotions that threatened to spin loose inside her.

"Thank you, it would be very ki—that is, I would welcome the opportunity to meet with the Bridges beforehand."

She started for the door, but his voice stopped her with a single word of soft entreaty. "Maeve . . . ?"

She turned to him, unable to prevent her response.

He stood in the glow of candlelight. For a moment, the harsh lines fell away from his face, so that he looked confused, as if he were struggling with some words that would not come to him, with some emotion he could not understand. He started to stretch out a hand to her, to take a step toward her.

Tension crackled in the air between them, snapping like

a rope stretched so tight that its strands were breaking, and she froze still, trapped by his stare.

The moment passed. He looked away and folded his hands behind him, and his face resumed its normal frown. "I would prefer to tell Dorothy and Clarissa that you are leaving us after you make a final decision in Bath."

She nodded, her mouth as dry as ashes. "As you wish."

Maeve turned and started for the door. Her dark dressing gown blended with the night, leaving only the flash of white from the hem of her nightgown as a guide to where she was.

Andrew glanced around the empty room, not even knowing what he was looking for. Oh, Lord, he had meant to tell her tonight about how those damnable dreams about music had stopped.

He glanced down at the carpet where she had sat. She had forgotten her candle to light her way back to her room. She had forgotten her slippers as well.

He picked them up. They were tiny and worn. The roses embroidered on the tops had frayed on the edges. He turned and stepped toward where she had disappeared in the darkness, thinking he would take the slippers to her. He would tell her all the things he had thought to tell her over the next few months.

But he could not take another step.

What would he tell her? Even now the words welled up inside him and lodged in his chest and throat and would not come. His thoughts wrecked like a ship against a wall of rock that lay inside him somewhere.

Maeve, he thought, and her name echoed inside him like a prayer in an empty cathedral.

He came to her in her dreams. She stirred restless in her sleep, awareness exciting her body with the fantasy her mind had begun to weave.

He came to her in the ruined wing and he asked her again to take down her braid, only this time when he asked, his eyes grew larger with excitement and interest. His mouth curved into an inviting smile, softening his face as she had so rarely seen it in the light of day. She pulled loose one ribbon and her hair tumbled free, and then his fingers shafted into its darkness, bunching it into his fists as he pulled her toward him. His mouth opened over hers, and she opened to him, muttering his name when his lips released hers to travel down her neck.

And then they were upon the carpet's softness, stripped bare already, and her hands traveled over the hard play of his muscles, seeking to give him the pleasure he gave her. For the first time in her life, she reveled in the knowledge that had cost her so dearly to learn, for now she could use it on him . . . for him.

His hand covered her breast, and in her sleep she gave a moan of pleasure.

"Yes, please . . . like that," her mind whispered to him. She twisted in her sheets and smiled up at him, watching desire darken his eyes until they were so black and large that she thought she could fall into them and never reach the end of their depths. She stroked his face, smoothing the frown as she had always wanted to, but as she could not dare in waking life.

And then his face changed—it sharpened, dark eyes lightened, and another man's face stared at her with a mocking grin.

Maeve woke with a small strangled scream.

She sat up in her empty bedroom, staring around her, her eyes wide. Andrew wasn't there. Neither was any other man. That was all long ago. That was all never to be.

But she stayed awake the rest of the night, her knees pulled up to her chin, unable to trust her sleep.

No wonder old women preached against the dangers

of the loss of innocence to young girls. How much worse it was this time to love a man—and to have the awareness of what her body craved from his.

She knew then that she must leave, no matter what the Bridges were like. She must, for she could not afford to compromise herself a second time.

Fourteen

Andrew stopped on the top step of Rothe House and frowned at the chaos stretched across the graveled drive. A massive black traveling coach stood before the steps, a team of four sturdy but unmatched chestnut and gray horses jingling their harness as they stamped their hooves and tossed their heads. A second carriage stood behind the first—this one with only a pair of bays attached and without a crest emblazoned on its doors. Trunks lay strapped upon the roofs of both vehicles, and servants fussed over the harness straps or struggled to fit just one more valise, one more bandbox either onto or into one of the two carriages. He had not seen so much traveling luggage strewn about since the French had fled Madrid, leaving in their wake nearly an equal amount of rubbish.

He turned as Lady Rothe came out of the house in a gray walking dress, struggling to tie a black-trimmed bonnet over her curls while clutching one of her lapdogs in the crook of her arm. Her other two black-and-white King Charles spaniels danced around her, their fat bodies wiggling.

Andrew had not counted on Lady Rothe's desire to make this journey, but she had taken it into her head that her ankle needed bathing in the healing Bath waters.

"Bringing the household with you?" he asked dryly.

She missed his sarcasm. "Oh, heavens, no. Just a few comforts we will need. Sheets of course. And some plate to eat upon." She turned and called into the house, "Hurry, Clarissa, dear, we must get an early start."

Andrew's mouth curled derisively. If half-ten in the morning was her notion of early, he must remember never to allow her a late start or it would take the better part of a month to reach Bath. On the other hand, he was not in a rush to hurry Maeve to a new employer.

His smiled softened. "Take your time, Dorothy. You must remember your recent invalid status and not push yourself."

She glanced at him, suspicious.

He merely smiled back at her.

A week of restless nights had fixed one notion in his mind: Maeve could be made to forget this nonsense of taking another position. He had thought it out as he would a campaign, and he had his strategy mapped.

It was her damnable pride that drove her to think of even accepting this position in a family with six girls. Six! My God, the work alone would wear her to the bone. So she must be made to understand how much more pleasant it would be for her to remain. She could be made to see that having Dorothy around was still no replacement for Maeve's strict supervision of Clarissa. He had until Bath was reached to impress this upon her, and perhaps a day or so more, and he refused to contemplate the possibility that he might fail. He was going to have things back as they ought to be, by damn.

Frowning, tapping his riding crop against his leg, he spared a brief moment to wonder just why Maeve's continued presence should matter so much to him. It was a question that had kept him pacing in his own room every night this past week, and had distracted him from the job of managing his estate.

He had not yet found an answer, other than who else would smile at his jokes? Damnation, he would miss those smiles. He liked how they always started with a glimmer in her gray eyes, and then the corners of her mouth would lift . . . and he wished—

"My lord?" a groom asked, interrupting Andrew's thoughts.

He swung around, irritated, and snapped, "Yes, what is it?"

"It's just . . . we're ready to leave, my lord."

Andrew bellowed a summons to Clarissa.

Five minutes later the girl ran out the front doors, her bonnet dangling by its ribbons and loose around her neck, her gray kitten, Jane, poking its head from a wicker basket clutched in her arms.

"I am sorry, but Jane would not come out until Miss Midden thought to tempt her with some milk."

"And where is Miss Midden?" Andrew asked, his temper strained and forgetting that he was trying to make this an unusually pleasant outing for everyone.

"Here, my lord," Maeve said from the doorway.

He glanced at her. His frown deepened to a scowl.

She stood before him in a dress he had not seen before. It was something in a dark blue fabric that made her eyes look more blue than gray.

It was a traveling dress, that much was obvious from the small jacket she wore over it, unbuttoned and loose. But rather than fitting too snug and straining at the seams as had her brown dress, this one did something else altogether. This dress outlined her form, emphasizing her slim figure and calling attention to her small, high breasts. Something gauzy and semi-transparent fell from her throat to the low-cut neckline, which curved down to offer distracting glimpses of the soft swell of those breasts. A lick of heat flickered through him.

He pulled his gaze back to her face. It rankled that she had bothered to wear a new dress only when she was thinking of leaving him.

"Where is your brown dress?" he asked. "And why have I never seen this one before?"

"Oh, that," Clarissa said, glancing up from her struggles to keep Jane in her basket. "I made it up for her. Doesn't it look well, Uncle?"

Maeve looked up and offered a hesitant smile, which faltered. "You don't like it?"

"Not at all. It's . . . it's different." He winced inwardly at how badly that had been done. "At least that bonnet of yours is gone. This new . . . what is it, straw? It's much better."

Her expression went wooden, and he decided he had better leave off before he dug himself a grave with his graceless tongue.

"Bath," Clarissa said, letting out a sigh and putting her cheek close to Jane's mewing face. "We are going to Bath!"

Maeve gladly turned her attention from Lord Rothe to Clarissa. Excitement shimmered in the girl's voice and glowed in her eyes. She was a pretty girl, but at this moment the beauty of the woman she would become took Maeve's breath away.

The worry rose in Maeve suddenly that Lady Rothe would not be vigilant enough with Clarissa when they went to London next year. Then Maeve glanced at Lord Rothe's scowling face. That expression alone would frighten off eligible as well as ineligible suitors. And Clarissa would soon no longer be her responsibility.

Lady Rothe leaned out from the traveling coach. "We shall never get anywhere if you dawdlers do not move along."

Clarissa hurried forward and Maeve started after her.

Lord Rothe's deep, quiet voice stopped her. "Miss Midden?"

She turned, her eyebrows raised with a question, her heart beating faster than it should. Now what did he dislike about her this morning? He had been nothing but surly since she had told him she would leave, and she was starting to resent it.

"You look lovely," he said. Then he turned, clapped his hat on his head and made for the horse he was to ride beside the carriage.

Maeve stared after him, desolate. The impulse to sit down on the steps of Rothe House and cry a river almost overcame her before she pulled her scraps of pride together and started for the carriage.

Dear Lord, this was going to be the longest journey of her life!

A small scratching on Maeve's door made her glance up from her tatting and ask who was there.

They had arrived in Bath, at the house that Lord Rothe had rented in the Royal Crescent, overlooking the greenery of Barton Fields. He had written ahead to ask his secretary, who was in the neighborhood, to acquire accommodations, and now Maeve sat in a comfortably furnished room, already feeling lost and disoriented. Her body still swayed and rocked from the carriage, and the faintest of headaches tightened her brow.

In response to Maeve's call, Clarissa came into the room, juggling a candle in one hand and her gray kitten in the other.

"My dear, do put one of those down before you singe Jane's fur or before she sets the house on fire by batting at the flame," Maeve said, already on her feet and taking the candle.

The girl plopped down on Maeve's bed.

It had taken eight exhausting days to make the trip to Bath, for Lady Rothe would not allow the team to do more than a brisk trot. Thankfully, Clarissa could read while traveling, and two of Mrs. Radcliffe's novels had

made conversation unnecessary. Maeve had been able to
sit and stare out the window, and had tried very hard not
to watch Lord Rothe.

He rode as would anyone who had spent years doing
just that. He rode as if molded onto the horse, his seat in
perfect balance, his hand light upon the rein, his back
straight and tall. Those glimpses of him ate away at
Maeve's determination, as did the evenings when he
seemed to exert himself to be more talkative than usual,
entertaining them all with stories of Spain and army life.

But she had already sent a note to Mrs. Bridges, fearing
that if she did not do so at once, her resolve would fail
her. And now she was due to see that lady tomorrow
morning.

She put away her half-finished lace collar and managed
a smile for Clarissa. "Too excited to sleep?"

Clarissa curled up on Maeve's bed. "Too homesick."
She glanced down at the kitten in her lap. "Isn't it silly?
For ages I yearn to leave, and now I am gone I miss it
terribly."

Maeve came to sit next to Clarissa. She dangled the
corded tassel of her dressing gown for Jane's amusement.
"It will pass. Tomorrow you shall be too busy to miss
anything. And it is good practice for when your uncle
takes you to London next year."

Clarissa scooted around on the bed and faced Maeve.
"You like him, don't you?" Maeve's hand gave a small
jerk. She pretended she had done it to pull the robe-tassel
away from Jane's sharp claws, as Clarissa went on. "I
mean, at least it seemed back home that you did, but these
past few days . . . well, it seems as if you have been
avoiding him. I mean, you are ever so polite at meals,
but I never see you laughing together as you used to at
home."

Maeve's hands stilled. "No. No, we cannot be as we
were at Rothe House."

"Why not? Whatever do you mean by that?"

Jane batted a paw on Maeve's hand for attention. Maeve settled the kitten on the bed and took Clarissa's hands. "My dear, the one thing that is a constant in life is that things change. The current of life carries us along with it, and sometimes we must let go of things we love to move along with that current."

Clarissa's eyes began to darken. "Move along? Who must move along? Oh, you mean yourself. You are leaving us?"

"Your uncle asked me to wait until I was certain, but I think it best that we both know we have to make the most of what time we have together." Maeve explained about the Bridges, forcing a cheerful optimism that was the exact opposite of the leaden weight in her chest.

Clarissa's expression tensed with anger and hurt, until she finally blurted out in childish petulance, "But I need you! Uncle hired you for me!" She pulled away and jumped off the bed, her eyes stormy, her lips trembling. "I won't have it! I'll tell Uncle you must stay."

Maeve held her tongue and waited for the storm to pass.

Finally, Clarissa's demands led to tears and then to breathless confusion. The girl's shoulders sagged as she asked, her tone softening, "Why must you go? Why can't you marry Uncle and stay with us?"

Shock left Maeve unable to move. Then a fierce wave of anger at how cruel and taunting those words were drove her to her feet and quickened her steps as she crossed the floor. Her fingers dug into Clarissa's shoulders. "You must never say that. Never!"

Clarissa's face blanched. "I . . . I'm sorry."

Maeve clutched the girl to her in a hug. "Oh, my dear, I'm the one who should be sorry. It is only myself I am angry with. But you must not speak of such things when you know nothing of the situation." She held Clarissa away. "My dear, your uncle is a fine gentleman, but he is a lord. He has a duty to his name and his station. You know how much duty matters to him. And I . . . well, I am not a suitable choice. And you must leave it at that."

Maeve could say no more to the girl. It was her responsibility to shield Clarissa from the unpleasant aspects of life. She could not expose her shameful past to this innocent girl.

Clarissa said nothing, but a mulish look came into her eyes and her chin took on a stubborn tilt. Maeve gave the girl another hug and then went to fetch Jane, who had hidden herself under the pillows. She handed the kitten back to Clarissa, who started to leave, her steps dragging and her face sullen.

At the door, Clarissa paused. "Uncle Andrew said I might go to the Assembly rooms, to a concert this week. You won't leave us until after that, will you? I mean, Mama has her own friends to visit, and if you do not go, then I shall not be able to, so please say you will stay that long at least?"

Maeve hesitated, but the tug from those enormous pleading eyes and the wistful tone tore apart her resolutions as if they were made of fairy dust. *It is for Clarissa, not because I want to stay*, she told herself as she gave in to Clarissa's request. And she knew that was the worst lie she had ever told anyone.

Maeve called upon Mrs. Bridges on Wednesday. Everything about the house—and Mrs. Bridges—seemed a touch overdone. She had a booming laugh, and a slight vulgarity to her in that she asked questions that had Maeve blushing. But when the woman brought out her daughters, love and warmth for every girl apparent in her ruddy face, Maeve could not help but warm to her.

The Bridges girls took after their mother in their plump

forms and round faces. They ranged from a talkative girl of twelve to a babe in arms. Maeve knew she would never feel fully at ease with Mrs. Bridges, but she saw how there could be a lifetime of satisfaction in seeing these girls grown and settled in their own lives. Maeve left at the end of an hour with Mrs. Bridges's offer in her head and no reason not to take such a perfect position.

Well, you have what you wished for, she told herself as she pasted a smile on her face. But why did the years ahead stretch forward so bleakly?

Lord Rothe had sent her to the interview in his carriage, and now she traveled back to the Royal Crescent in comfort. She stared out at the elegant white stone buildings of Bath, all built to please the eye with classical grace, and she wished deeply that she had their indifference. A heart was only a curse, she decided.

At the hired house, she was a little surprised that a servant did not anticipate her arrival and open the door for her. She shrugged off the oversight and untied the ribbons to her straw bonnet as she started up the stairs.

The faint sound of music made her stop and turn. She hesitated, then began to follow the chiming notes. They led her to one of the rooms just off the main hall. The door stood open and so she glanced inside.

Lord Rothe stood before a mahogany table, his hand on top of an open square rosewood box. A music box, Maeve realized, charmed by the tune, but her heart tightened at what a poor substitute this must be for the music he once had been able to create with his own hands.

He glanced up suddenly, and heat flooded into Maeve's face for intruding. "I beg your pardon, I . . . I was just going upstairs to see if Lady Rothe needed me and I heard—"

"Dorothy and Clarissa have gone out." He smiled. "The lure of shops could not be ignored, so I sent both the footmen with them, but they'll probably need a dozen more to carry their acquisitions back."

Andrew kept his smile in place and tried to speak lightly. He knew she had been to see Mrs. Bridges. The apprehension created by such knowledge lay tight around his chest, restrictive as a dress parade uniform. He had made a point of it to be here alone when she returned. He had planned to offer his condolences for the Bridges not being what she had wanted. He had willed himself only to think on the possibility that Maeve would not take the position.

Now he searched her eyes, for those gray depths gave away too much of her thoughts, and the band around his chest contracted until all that remained was a dull ache. For he saw regret, unhappiness and her damn stubborn determination.

She had made up her mind to go.

He glanced down at the music box. "I have no idea why Dorothy brought this along. It was my mother's. I think it was my father who gave it to Dorothy as a wedding present. It must be one of her comforts she dragged with us from Rothe House." He had no idea why he was blathering on about a music box. Perhaps it was because he had nothing else to say. He had run out of words. Out of arguments.

God, he had not felt this bad after the worst day in Spain.

He closed the lid to the box, shutting off the wistful melody.

Maeve came into the room. "We never did have our dance."

He glanced at her, frowning.

"Our dance?" she reminded him. She took off the jacket for her blue walking dress. Under the gauzy material at the neckline, he could see her breasts rise with uneven breaths. She offered a hesitant smile. "You did say that you had forgotten how to dance."

She came across the room, her swaying hips outlined by the soft fall of the fabric of her dress. He opened the music box again, moving without thought, not once looking away from her. He stared down into her eyes and held out his hand as he asked, his tone formal, "Miss Midden, may I have this dance?"

Her eyes lit with a glow. She started to reach out to take his hand, and then she looked down at the music box, her expression falling apart.

"What is it?" he asked, taking an instinctive step toward her.

She looked up at him, her eyes distressed. "The music. I don't know how to waltz. I never learned."

He laughed then. At the utter absurdity of the situation. At himself. At a fate which denied him even the simplest of indulgences with her.

He closed the music box and gave her a rueful smile. The distress had left her face, but her gray eyes remained shadowed.

"We are quite a pair, are we not? A lord who cannot act a lord and a governess who cannot teach dance."

She folded her hands before her. She did not smile, but some of the glow came back to her eyes. "A governess is not required to give instruction in dance steps, and you cannot continue to claim you do not feel like Lord Rothe, for you've quite mastered a true aristocratic command."

He stopped smiling. "But not well enough that I can exert my influence over you."

She went to pick up her jacket.

He could not let her leave, so he blurted out, "Maeve, I can only ask you one last time. Why will you not stay with us?"

He knew this desperate last action was doomed, but

the dogged persistence left over from his military days would not allow him to give up the fight.

She kept her face averted, so that he had her profile with its straight nose and determined chin to study and memorize.

Maeve bit the inside of her cheek to keep from blurting out her reasons. She dared not speak. If she began with how she felt, then she would have to explain other things. Her stomach knotted at that thought, for what if she told him and he turned away from her in shame and disgust, just as her own father had?

Andrew watched the emotions that flickered in her eyes, and how she pressed her mouth into a tight line as if to keep something back.

He folded his hands behind his back to keep himself from reaching out to touch her, and he asked, "Is there something which affects your decision?"

Her chin lifted. She faced him, her expression utterly controlled. "There is nothing else I have to say. I shall be leaving at the end of the week. Thank you for all you have done for me."

She started out. At the door, she stopped. "I am sorry we did not have that dance." And then she was gone.

Andrew sat down. He rested his elbows on his knees and stared at the room around him, not seeing it, unable to take in the reality of the moment, unable to acknowledge what had happened.

Then he buried his face in his hands.

"Miss Midden, you aren't going to wear that old thing?" Clarissa said, her dismay echoing down the halls.

Maeve paused and turned to greet her charge for the evening, and then she said with a smile, "I cannot wear the traveling dress you made me, however lovely it is.

And the black is quite suitable for a concert. Besides, who will look at me with you there to stare at?"

Maeve took pride in the girl's appearance. She had persuaded both Clarissa and Lady Rothe into adopting the simplest designs of dress for Clarissa. Something suitable for a girl who had lost her father within the past year. Something to make her look older. She wore a dark gray silk gown, embroidered around the neck and hem in black. Her gold hair had been pulled up into soft curls that framed her heart-shaped face, and which played up the perfection of her features. She looked lovely.

However, Maeve's flattery did not distract Clarissa. She folded her arms and said, "I'm not going. Not if you wear that. You look like my . . . my governess."

Lady Rothe stepped into the hall, and Clarissa turned to her. "Mother, you must talk to her. Tell her she cannot go out in that . . . that shroud!"

Lady Rothe paused and stared at Maeve, who tried not to fidget as her ladyship's blue eyes swept over her, as shrewd and evaluating as a horse dealer's summation at an auction.

"Oh, heavens, no, of course she cannot. Did we not buy something for you, Miss Midden, when we went shopping?"

"Mother, Miss Midden did not go shopping with us today. But why can she not wear one of your older dresses? You had that lovely black lace gown made just after Father died, and you never wore it."

Maeve had an image of herself lost and swimming in the yards of fabric of one of Lady Rothe's dresses. "Clarissa, I don't think I could fill your mother's dresses as well as she does."

Lady Rothe's chin rose. "I was not always this large. And my friend Mrs. Green, with whom I am to dine tonight, swears that if I take the waters I might regain much of my youthful figure. Why, she herself has lost nearly four stone. But as to the dress, I did not pack any of my older dresses, Clarissa. So it cannot be thought of."

Clarissa's eyes turned limpid. "Mother, by the sheerest accident my maid packed your black lace, thinking it was mine. And so we must try it on Miss Midden."

"Clarissa . . . ," Maeve began, frowning at the girl, not quite certain what Clarissa was up to, but suspecting some scheme was afoot.

Blissfully ignoring everything, as if none of it mattered, Clarissa took hold of Maeve's hand so that she had no choice but to follow.

Between Clarissa's coaxing and Lady Rothe's insistence, Maeve allowed them to talk her into a revealing black lace gown, which had obviously been made for a much smaller Lady Rothe.

It fit suspiciously well, in fact. Too well. Maeve turned from her reflection in the glass to look at Clarissa. "I could vow that it looks as well on me as the blue traveling dress you made," she said, making clear that she suspected Clarissa had once again been busy with her too clever needle.

Clarissa beamed. "Yes, isn't that the greatest luck?"

Lady Rothe stared at the gown in astonishment. "It is amazing. The dressmaker must have taken my measurements all wrong, for this never would have fit—"

"Mother, aren't you going to be late for dinner with Mrs. Green?" Clarissa took her mother's arm and started for the door.

Maeve glanced at her reflection and tugged up on the low-cut bodice. She had not worn anything so daring in years. She twirled, letting the gray satin undergown swirl against her legs. She would have had to be the most ungrateful woman in the world not to go along with something Clarissa had worked so hard to achieve. She would just have to hope that this dress was the only surprise Clarissa had planned for this evening.

Clarissa came back from escorting her mother out of the house, and then Maeve and Clarissa descended the stairs.

Lord Rothe waited for them in the entry hall, frowning over a letter.

"Uncle," Clarissa called out, and then cleared her throat.

Maeve gave the girl a quelling glance, but Clarissa merely smiled and called out, "I hope it is not bad news you have, Uncle."

"No, simply a letter from Edward, my secretary. You'd think the fellow could get . . ." He looked up, and his dark eyes widened in astonishment.

Andrew came to the base of the stairs, his letter, with its nonsense about an older and a younger Miss Midden, already forgotten.

She had never worn such a dress at Rothe House, and this one, cut low to expose the graceful curve of her neck, revealing flawless white skin, struck him like the repercussion of a cannon's fire. Sweat broke out on his hands, and his heart kicked up to battle speed. The high waist of the gown pushed up the soft swell of her breasts for any man to ogle—as he was doing now, he realized.

Andrew frowned, angry that now that she had made up her mind to leave, she paraded around like . . . well, like a too desirable woman.

"What's wrong?" Maeve asked.

He glanced at her, and shame for his churlish thoughts swept through him. The answer was obvious as to why she would not have dressed in this fashion before now: He had never given her the opportunity. At Rothe House she had been Miss Midden, the unseen companion.

"Is it something in the letter?" Clarissa asked, worry creeping into her voice. "Will we not be able to go out tonight?"

He caught a flicker of regret in Maeve's eyes before

she could suppress it. An idea began to form. If he had learned anything from his commander in chief of the Peninsular War, it was how to regroup from a defeat and come back to fight again. He was not yet done with Miss Midden.

"Yes, I'm afraid I'll be unable to join you tonight. But, please, you must go without me." He stared directly at his niece and tried to put as much meaning in his tone as he could without alerting Maeve. "Clarissa, I'm certain you will display tonight how little you need a chaperon."

Clarissa stared back at him, her eyes blank. Just as he began to think she would not take the hint, a glint of wicked mischief set to dancing in her eyes, like the fire in fine sapphires. She answered with demure deference, "Of course, Uncle Andrew."

A small shudder chased along his spine. Well, he had thrown his good Christian Maeve to a lion tonight. Now she would see just how much she *was* needed.

He watched them depart, Clarissa practically dragging Maeve out with her. Then he turned back to his puzzling letter.

Just what the devil did Edward mean there were two Miss Middens?

At the first interval, Maeve glanced around for Clarissa, wondering where the girl had gone. She had been all chattering high spirits when they had arrived, and Maeve had started to worry as soon as they entered the room. Clarissa could talk about nothing but the gentlemen present and began flirting in a manner that nearly caused Maeve to drag the girl away. When she gave Clarissa a warning, the girl merely smiled sweetly, apologized . . . and five minutes later started casting eyes at yet another fellow.

Maeve began to wonder if Lord Rothe's concern for his niece's ability to behave in public was actually well-grounded. Would Lady Rothe be able to manage Clarissa and make her act like the demure miss that society expected? Or would Clarissa carry on like this every time she slipped away from her uncle's stern control?

Worry for Clarissa knotted in Maeve like a tangled skein of yarn, but she was not supposed to trouble herself with such things now. She had given her notice, and by this time tomorrow she would have said her good-byes to the Derhurst family.

But she did not want her time with them to end with a disaster.

Exasperated, Maeve decided she would drag Clarissa bodily from the concert if she must before the girl disgraced herself.

Bath's Lower Assembly rooms were not large. The high ceilings, decorated with white plaster trim to balance the colored walls, offered excellent acoustics. Just now the hum of voices, the laughter of ladies and gentlemen, echoed into a roar that would have drowned out the rush of the River Avon over the weir beside Pulteney Bridge.

Maeve glanced around, ignoring the smiles sent her way by gentlemen. She was not here to flirt. Neither was Clarissa.

Finally the crowd parted slightly, and Maeve saw the girl near the refreshment table. Clarissa was talking to a man who stood with his back toward Maeve. She spared the briefest of glances at the fellow, taking in only his thinning blond hair and thickening waist, which both suggested he was far too old for Clarissa.

She started toward the pair, and then recognition hit her. She looked back at the man and the world fell out from under her. It could not be. He had always said he despised Bath. Yet there he stood, flirting with Clarissa.

Fury fired Maeve's blood. *How dare he?*

Along with the fury came panic and fear. *What was he telling Clarissa?*

She hurried forward to get Clarissa away from this man—the man who had ruined her.

Fifteen

Andrew sat in the drawing room, studying the letter from his secretary. The more he read it, the more perplexed he grew. What was all this about two Miss Middens and one school? It did not make sense. Maeve had told him she had no siblings. Could there have been an aunt who had run the school with her? And was this woman still alive?

There was only one way to get an immediate answer. Edward had posted this riddle of his from Bristol, where he was overseeing the shipment of building materials for the ruined wing at Rothe House. Bristol lay but a dozen or so miles from Bath. With the full moon and some luck, he could be in Bristol within three hours, and back in Bath for breakfast.

Andrew rose, dragged on the bellpull, and when the butler arrived, gave orders to have a horse ready for him within the hour. If nothing else, it would give him a chance to do something, for it was damnably hard to sit and wait to see if Clarissa had done her part tonight.

Vincent Deprie had never lacked for address, nor for sheer nerve, Maeve decided as he actually bowed and greeted her as if they had not last parted with bitter words and hate between them.

"Maeve, how good to see you. Why, never tell me,

Miss Derhurst, that this is the duenna you spoke of, the dragon guarding you tonight? I cannot credit that, for Maeve is—"

"I am not pleased to see you, Vincent. If you had any decency—"

"Ah, but I never did," he said, giving her an infuriating wink and a roguish smile, turning her comment into a joke.

She ached to slap him, but she could not do so in public, not without drawing unseemly attention to Clarissa. She could only take some satisfaction in that the years had been unkind to him. His golden hair now lay thin and receding from his high forehead. His tall form—once romantically slim—had thickened, and his tight-fitting coat and pantaloons emphasized his expanding girth. His pale eyes, which she had once thought intriguing, she now found shifty and as shallow as a village pond.

She loathed him. But his glance at her mocked her, daring her to say something about their shared past. *I know you intimately*, he seemed to say every time he looked at her. *I know you will keep quiet, for I will expose you if you dare to expose me.*

It made her hate him even more that he knew her weakness, her fear of exposure.

So she stood next to Clarissa and stared daggers at him.

"Tell me, how is it that you know Miss Midden?" Clarissa asked, glancing from Vincent to Maeve.

"It was a long time ago that we met. In London, was it not, Maeve?"

"London? But I thought you disliked that city, Miss Midden." Clarissa began to ask something else, but an acquaintance of Mr. Deprie claimed his attention.

Maeve took the opportunity to whisper to Clarissa, her voice urgent, "This man is not someone you should know."

Clarissa looked back, her brows arched and her eyes innocent. "You know him, so why should not I?"

"He is a rake. He ruins young girls such as you for his own gain." Clarissa opened her mouth to protest, but Maeve cut her off. "I know—your godmama swears that rakes make the best husbands, but she forgot to add that rakes hardly ever marry the girls they ruin. Not unless there is a fortune in it for them!"

A worried look flashed across Clarissa's eyes, but then she tossed her curls. "But I have a fortune," she said, and turned back to Vincent Deprie with a smile.

Maeve nearly walked off, leaving the both of them to each other, but she could not abandon her duty. Nor could she abandon the headstrong Clarissa. The girl did not know how cruel the world could be.

Fortunately, the signal went out that the second half of the concert was about to begin. Maeve took Clarissa's hand. "Excuse us, Mr. Deprie. We must resume our seats."

His pale blue eyes hardened and his voice took on the faintest of threats. "But you must allow me to escort you."

And if you don't, you will regret it, his cold stare told her. Then he was laughing with Clarissa and had her arm in his, and Maeve had no choice but to follow them, and no choice but to sit next to them as Vincent claimed a chair beside Clarissa's.

Maeve sat listening to the music with hands tightly clutched together, her fingers cold, struggling for some way to get rid of him, or for some excuse to take Clarissa away. She had always feared meeting him again. She had dreaded it. But her nightmares had been woven around meeting him and finding that the hideous attraction she had once felt for him still commanded her.

Now, she realized she was no longer at risk.

But Clarissa . . . ah, she was so young, so inexperienced. Just as she herself had once been.

The music changed, and Maeve found herself distracted by the next tune, its words speaking to her as if to no one else. *I have a silent sorrow here. A grief I'll ne'er impart. It breathes no sigh, it sheds no tear. But it consumes my heart . . .*

Maeve listened to the song, transfixed by its longing, trapped by the simple melody.

The music ended at last, everyone applauded and rose, and the crowd pressed for the exits, for the rooms had grown stifling hot. Maeve blinked and came back to herself, shaking off the mood induced by the poignant lyrics. She glanced around to tell Clarissa that it was time to go.

The girl was nowhere to be found.

Panic filled Maeve with frantic energy. She looked around her but could not see Clarissa's golden hair, nor Vincent's repellent form.

"Clarissa," she called out, but the hum of the crowd made her call just another noise. She pushed through the crowd as she struggled to gain the exit. *Dear God, please let her be safe.*

Fifteen minutes later the rooms had nearly cleared. Maeve pressed a shaking hand over her stomach. Then she saw Clarissa in the hallway. Maeve hurried forward, searching the girl's face, looking for some sign of panic or alarm. Clarissa's curls were rumpled and she tugged her dress back up on one shoulder, but she seemed calm. No tears. No flush of remorse. Perhaps the crowd had disordered her appearance.

"Clarissa," Maeve said, catching up to her side. "What happened to you? Are you all right?"

Clarissa merely smiled. "Don't be such a goose. Of course I am. I have you here with me." She tucked her arm into Maeve's. "Wasn't that a lovely evening? And Mr. Deprie . . . so worldly. He is old, of course, but no more so than Uncle. And such address. Do you know, he reminded me strongly of that gentleman we saw in York . . . only older, of course."

"Were you with him? Did he accost you?"

"My dear Miss Midden, what could happen to me in a crowded room?"

Maeve found that answer unsatisfying, but it was the only one Clarissa would give.

When they arrived back at the rented house in the Royal Crescent, Clarissa made a great show of stifling her yawns and went to her bed at once, muttering a sleepy good night. Maeve considered for a moment asking the hired butler if Lord Rothe was still awake, or if her ladyship had returned, but she felt shy suddenly. She did not know this fellow, and a moment gave her time to reconsider, for what would she say to either his lordship or Clarissa's mother? She could not announce that Clarissa had made the acquaintance of a disreputable fellow, not without having to drag in more explanations than she felt capable of providing.

So instead she bade the butler good night and climbed the stairs to her room.

She could find no reason to feel uneasy, yet she lay in her bed for hours staring at the dark ceiling, her mind restless and her emotions tight in her chest as if some demon lay upon her, whispering evil thoughts into her ear.

Finally, sleep began to weigh on her eyes, and her rational mind smoothed over her feelings. After all, how much harm could Vincent have done in just one meeting?

The next morning, she discovered exactly how much damage a man as evil as Vincent could cause.

Her answer came in the form of a letter, delivered by a maid who curtsied and said that Miss Derhurst had asked for this note to be given to Miss Midden when she came down to breakfast, or at seven of the clock exactly.

Maeve recognized Clarissa's hand. She scanned the note, her coffee and food forgotten. Then she rose to drag so hard on the bellpull that she heard it ringing in the servants' quarter. The hired butler hurried in, and she demanded, "When did Miss Derhurst leave the house?"

"Leave, miss?"

"Yes, leave. Are you deaf as well as blind? Oh, it is no matter. Is Lord Rothe in?"

"No, miss. He left last night on urgent business. I believe, however, he does intend to return later in the day."

Maeve cursed herself. Why had she not warned Clarissa? Why had she not sat up and kept guard? It had taken Vincent longer than one night to seduce her away from her family, but not much longer—and she had been just as smitten with him in only one night.

Distracted, she pushed her hair back with one hand and tried to push back the memories as well as the regrets. Neither would save Clarissa.

She turned to the puzzled butler, Clarissa's note crumpled in her hand. At least Clarissa had been beyond foolish—she had written the name of an inn in the nearby town of Devizes where she was to meet with Deprie to elope with him. There was yet a chance to save the girl.

"Summon a carriage at once," Maeve commanded. "I cannot wait. I want a post-chaise and four, not a hack, and if it is here within a quarter hour, there's a guinea for you as well as for the post boys!"

The butler's eyes brightened. "Yes, miss," he said, bowing and already half out the door.

Maeve ran up to her room to collect her bonnet and her savings. She still had the ten-pound banknote Lord Rothe had given her, as well as three guineas and two shillings which she had set aside from her last position. A post-chaise and four might cost her as much as three shillings a mile, so heaven help her if she had to travel more than sixty miles. But Devizes could not be more than twenty miles away . . . so she must pray that she might yet catch them at the inn there, or at least learn news of where they were bound.

She ran downstairs, started to hunt for paper and pen to leave a note, but the butler called out, himself breathless, that the chaise was here. Maeve left at once, calling out to the butler to tell Lord Rothe and Lady Rothe that she and Clarissa had gone out for the day.

A little over an hour later, Maeve's chaise and four drew up to the sign of the Black Bear on the south side of Devizes' market square. Maeve climbed out, her teeth aching from clenching them, her stomach churning, and her anger flaming high.

"Where is Mr. Deprie?" she demanded as soon as she laid eyes on the innkeeper.

That worthy looked her up and down, his own eyes narrowing. "Quality . . . always summat rum with their goings-on." He jerked a thumb, indicating a room at the back of a hallway. "If it's the towheaded gent you want, you'll find him at the back in me best parlor. And tell him not a drink does he get 'til I feel the weight of his purse," he yelled after Maeve as she strode down the narrow hallway toward the back of the inn.

Maeve braced herself as she threw open the door, ready for any scene of debauchery. Instead, she found Vincent lying on the couch, clutching his head.

"Where is she? Where is Clarissa?" she demanded, striding into the room and slamming the door shut behind her.

Sunlight slanted in from windows that looked into a back garden, casting golden rays across the floor. The sun illuminated a sparsely furnished room, and a gentleman who lay upon a velvet-covered couch, a red cloth pressed to his forehead.

Vincent opened one eye. His other eye, marred by purple discoloration, seemed to be rapidly swelling shut. "If you mean that amazon hoyden who masquerades as an innocent, I hope she's gone to perdition."

"Vincent, if you have done anything to her, I'll—"

"To her? By God, madam, it is I who's been done to!" He rose and swept an arm out. "Begged me to rescue her from that uncle of hers. Kissed me even. Thought the little baggage was practically panting for it. She named the inn even . . . and what does she do when she gets here? Hits me with God-knows-what and takes my purse with her, stranding me! I don't know what you're teaching these days, Maeve, but, by God, you at least ought to learn them not to thieve!"

Maeve gave him a grim smile. "She hit you? Well, then she knows more than I could ever teach her if she got your measure at a glance. But I doubt this was her idea—you tried your tricks with her, did you not? What, are willing girls with money so hard to find these days, Vincent? Or is it just your luck that you always get families who will not pay your price for their daughters?"

His hand dropped away from his head, and his face took on an ugly snarl. "Damn it, I ought to—"

"You ought to what?" Maeve asked, standing her ground. "What can you do to me that you have not already done?"

He smiled, but the expression twisted on his face to a sneer, and Maeve wondered how she had ever thought him handsome. "I can ruin you with a word. You and that doxy you have under your tutelage. I'll have the magistrate summoned and have you both before the dock for theft and whoring."

Anger fired in her veins. "Do please call the magistrate. And then I will do what I should have done years ago, Vincent. I will expose you as the contemptible seducer you are. You compromised my body with your pretenses of love, but I compromised my soul by fearing you, by trying to hide what you made me. What? No interest now in calling for the law? Well, then I will save you the trouble and summon him myself!"

She swung around and pulled open the door, starting to shout, "Landlord, I . . ."

But her words died, for as she swung the door wide, there stood Lord Rothe, his hand outstretched to grasp the latch, his dark face set in an implacable expression.

Maeve fell back a step before she could recover.

His lordship glanced at her once, and her heart skipped a beat. She had never seen anything so wonderful as him . . . nor so frightening. He was hatless, his hair wildly disordered, and he wore a dust-covered riding coat, breeches and tall boots, with—oddly—a sword buckled around his waist.

His dark eyes flashed as he strode into the room.

"Who the devil are you?" Vincent asked. "Get out. This is a private room."

Andrew took one look at the aging fop, one glance at Maeve's white face, and made an immediate decision. He advanced on the fop, his fist clenched. He struck without warning, and his right fist connected in a solid, satisfying blow that sent the fellow across the room. The fop hit the wall and slid to the floor.

Andrew strode over to where the man lay. "Get up."

The man on the floor felt his jaw and crouched lower. "You must be related to Maeve's girl."

Andrew knew that something must have flashed in his eyes, for the man on the floor flinched as if he expected to be hit while he lay there.

"Very well, stay where you are, you cur. You're no gentleman, so you don't merit treatment as such. But, by God, if you move without my saying so, I'll take exception and thrash you whether you are standing for it or not."

He turned to Maeve, who stood there wide-eyed and for once without words. "Now, what the devil is this? I get home from chasing across the county to unravel the story of whether you are Miss Midden who ran Miss Midden's Academy for Girls, or if you are not her but are in fact some relative or some pupil who inherited the place, and I find a letter from Clarissa about you being in danger. So I chase off here to find this fellow looking as if he wants to murder you, and you shouting for the landlord!"

"Clarissa!" Maeve groped her way to a chair and sat down, suddenly understanding that Vincent had been telling the truth for once. Clarissa had left letters for both her and Lord Rothe—she had oh so neatly arranged everything, including her own abduction and her own rescue.

"Oh, dear," Maeve said, feeling just a little light-headed. "I think you have actually been right about your niece all along. She really is not fit to be turned loose upon the world."

"Of course not, but what has that to do with this fellow?" he demanded. "I will have you know, Maeve, that I have not slept all night and am in no mood for long explanations. What is going on here?"

Maeve looked up into his thunderous face, a rush of feelings for him leaving her unable to speak for a moment. She dragged off her bonnet, and then his words sank in. She looked up at him, the old shame and fear trickling along her skin like ice water. "You've been asking about me? About Miss Midden's Academy for Girls?"

"Well, yes. What of it? I thought . . . well, truth be told, I thought it might provide me some clue, some information I could use to convince you to stay with Clarissa and go with us to London for her presentation at court. It seemed as if you had an unreasonable fear of society, and that the cause for that must lay in your past—

something perhaps you were ashamed of. I thought—like the arrogant fool I am—I could root it out like a weed."

"What an appropriate analogy," Vincent said, levering himself up on his elbow.

Lord Rothe shot him a look, his hand dropping to his saber hilt. "You, sir, may keep your mouth shut and will hereafter only speak if addressed. Am I understood?"

Vincent eyed the saber and sullenly nodded.

Maeve watched this interchange with a lightness in her that she had not felt in years. Ah, she had compromised herself with Vincent—but she had compromised herself even more with her shame. She had allowed fear to force her into a dishonesty she loathed. She had compromised herself by thinking that she could hide what she was. Well, it was time to stop pretending. It was time to stop such soul-killing compromises.

She stood up, strength flowing into her as if for years she had dragged around heavy chains and had just now let go of their weight. "My lord, there are certain things you should know about me . . . and my past. Clarissa may have exaggerated the danger I was in today, but this man did hurt me terribly at one time."

Lord Rothe's black eyes flashed. However, he merely said in a tight voice, "Go on. I'm listening."

Maeve swallowed the last tremble of fear, which shivered inside her more from habit than from any real sense that she was in any danger. She took a breath, determined to make a full confession. "I wish I could blame Vincent for everything, but, in truth, I was more than willing to throw my life away. I was very much like Clarissa—headstrong, certain I could handle anything. I was eighteen, and I thought I was in love.

"My father's disapproval did not matter to me. My mother was not there to guide either him or me. I acted, not with reason as I should have, but with an unwise heart. I threw myself into a decision that seemed romantic. I ran away with this man—Vincent Deprie."

Andrew's jaw tightened and his eyes narrowed. Maeve held her breath for a moment, but he said nothing. She walked to the window and looked outside. It was easier to tell the rest without looking at him.

"My father cut me off. I did not care. But then I learned that Vincent cared more for my family's money than he did for my person."

"I offered—" Vincent interrupted as he began to rise, but a cold glance from Lord Rothe cut off his words and he subsided.

Maeve turned and glared at the man she had once loved enough to ruin herself. "You kindly offered to keep me as your mistress, and not to discard me. But I would not have stayed with you then if you had begged me to marry you!"

She turned and faced Lord Rothe, pulling together all of her courage. She would be honest with him. She would see to it that Vincent never had the chance to ruin any other girl. It was what she should have done years ago.

"Vincent left me in London. I had nowhere to go. My relatives did not answer my letters. I saw my father but once in London, and he did not acknowledge me, but told me instead that his daughter was dead. The only kindness I found came from the real Miss Midden—my old schoolmistress. She took me in and gave me a position of trust, even knowing what she did about my past. She taught me how to turn my experience into wisdom, and she became like a mother to me. I cried for weeks when she died, but she left me an even greater gift in her school."

"She left you debts," Lord Rothe interrupted, his voice harsh and condemning.

Maeve smiled. "And should I have blamed her for the generous heart that led to such debts when I had benefited so much from it? I could not be so unkind. I wished only that she could somehow live on—she deserved a memorial. So I took on her school, and her name. But I was not up to the challenge. I could not stave off the creditors. After eighteen months, the school closed, and I took up the only profession I knew—teaching."

"Is your name Maeve?" Lord Rothe asked, stepping closer to her, a frown drawing his dark eyebrows together.

"Yes. I was Maeve Preston of Preston-Crowmarsh, in Oxfordshire. But I lost the right to that name long ago." She turned to Vincent. She no longer hated him. Now all she felt was scorn and pity. He lay on the floor, looking like the weak man he had always been. "And now I will see you prosecuted, Mr. Deprie, for the abduction of Miss Clarissa Derhurst."

"I think not," Lord Rothe said.

Maeve swung around. "What? But you can't mean to let him go."

"Can't I? If he's arrested for Clarissa's abduction, then she is ruined."

"Then I will see him arrested for what he did to me!"

Andrew came up to her and smiled sadly. "Would you have me watch you ruin your life a second time? Maeve, think a moment. You said that your Miss Midden taught you wisdom. Do not take this rash action; do not act just with your heart."

She stared at Vincent, who had started to look smug. "I won't see him go unpunished," she vowed.

"I didn't ask for that," Lord Rothe said.

She glanced at him. His smile was a flash of warmth for her alone, and then his face hardened and he strode over to Deprie.

"Get up," he said, and when Vincent sank lower, Lord Rothe grabbed him by the lapels and hauled him to his feet. "You are a sorry excuse for a man, Deprie. But you must have once had something to recommend you which

Maeve glimpsed and responded to, so for that reason I will not kill you on the spot. I give you a choice.

"Wellington is fond of saying that the English army is the scum of the Earth. It also, however, has been the making of many men. So you may enlist. There is a war in the colonies, after all, that needs patriotic souls, or at least cannon fodder."

"And if I refuse?" Vincent said, struggling to cling to some dignity and not cower.

Lord Rothe thrust him away, and then settled his hand on his sword. "I've killed men before; your death won't weigh heavy on me. And I shall use my power and title to buy a dozen witnesses who'll swear they saw a fair duel. That's your choice—and it's a sight more clemency than the courts of this land would ever grant you."

Maeve held her breath as Vincent's eyes shifted from Lord Rothe to her and back again. She could not believe Lord Rothe would kill Vincent—but his voice carried an unbending tone that sent a chill down her spine.

Warily, Vincent straightened. He smoothed his coat. "I've always thought I should do better in the Americas. More room for a man of my scope and vision."

The corner of Lord Rothe's mouth curled up, but his eyes were deadly as they rested on Vincent. Rothe strode to the door and shouted for the landlord. When the man came in, Rothe tossed him a gold coin. "You have a recruiting officer here, I expect. The town's large enough for it. And Mr. Deprie has a sudden burning desire to join up. But in the meantime, Mr. Deprie would like to enjoy the benefit of your cellars. I fear his courage may fail him before he signs up, and we don't want that to happen, do we, Mr. Deprie?"

Vincent's lip curled. "What about my bill here? I haven't any money."

"You won't need money aboard an army transport, Deprie." Lord Rothe counted out some coins for the landlord, who began to bow and throw "your lordships" in with every other phrase. "You will see he goes with the recruiting officer?" Rothe said.

The landlord grinned. He was a thickset man with hands that looked as if they could crush rocks. He took hold of Vincent Deprie's arm. " 'Course, yer lordship. I'll make sure, yer lordship."

Lord Rothe shut the door on the departing pair, then he turned to Maeve. "That is one problem solved. Now, what I am to do with a governess who was hired to control my niece—a companion who was to provide a chaperon—a woman who has instead nearly compromised my niece's reputation as well as her own?"

Maeve looked down and started to fold her hands docilely before her, but then she left them hanging limply at her sides. Her shoulders sagged. The energy that had roused her earlier seemed to have dissipated, like a fire that had consumed its fuel. He had every right to be angry with her. She had no defense against his charges.

"It seems so inadequate to say that I am sorry." She lifted her gaze, but kept her chin lowered. "I never dreamed my past might endanger Clarissa."

He sank into a chair, his saber rattling. He shoved it out of the way with an automatic gesture. He did not seem to realize that he had left her standing. He looked distracted, as if he did not even know where he was any longer.

"And did you ever think that I might be of aid to you? My God, Maeve, what kind of monster am I that you could not confide in me? You know me better than any person in this world, and yet you do not trust me? Did you think I would turn on you for what happened to you? Or even Clarissa—who deserves, honestly, to be locked up in a tower for this escapade—did you think I would give her the thrashing she deserves? Maeve, what do you think I am?"

"Oh, please don't say that. It is not you whom I did not trust. It was myself." She walked over to him, and the misery on his face cut into her. She knelt on the floor before him, her hands resting on his knees so that he had to look at her.

"Don't you see? I gave my heart once to a man who did not want it. I feared so very much that I was only repeating my own history. My own father rejected me after what I did. I could not believe that anyone would ever love me again. I could not trust myself, Andrew."

The sound of his name on her lips ripped through him like a rocket. Of all the people in the world, he could think of no one who more deserved to be loved. The desire for her—and to give her that love—bled out of his heart just as if that rocket had pierced him through. He took her face in his hands and smoothed his thumb across her lips as he had dreamed of doing.

"Maeve, oh, my dear, precious Maeve. I've been the coward here, not you. You were so right not to trust me before, for I went about like a blind fool, refusing to see what everyone else must have seen in your eyes. But I didn't want to see it. I was so afraid . . . I didn't even know how much I feared your rejection until this morning when I read that note from Clarissa. You've never seen a military man shake so from fear. And I knew then that the only thing I feared more than your rejection was losing you utterly."

She could not seem to speak, so he rose, pulling her to her feet as he did so, enfolding her in his arms. Something inside him burst loose, and like a falcon freed from his tethers, he soared at the sight of her soft, glowing eyes.

"God, Maeve, I have been such an idiot. I've lain awake at nights thinking of ways to keep you at Rothe House. And not for Clarissa's sake. Not for Dorothy. For me. And if you cannot trust your own feelings, you must trust mine. I want to marry you, Maeve. I want to love you."

"But my past, I am not—"

"Hush," he said, putting his finger over her lips to trace their curves again. "If you are going to start talking nonsense about not having dowries or not being pure, or not being what I need, I shall have to stoop to Vincent Deprie's habit of seduction. I want you, Maeve, make no mistake about that. But I want you because your mind and your heart want me as well. I'll accept no compromises about that."

"But—"

He kissed her to stop her excuses, kissed her as he had in his dreams, only this time her warm, giving mouth was a reality that transcended any fantasy. He deepened the kiss, both hating Deprie for being the first to teach her pleasure and blessing the scoundrel for being the catalyst that had brought her to save him. And then he forgot about Deprie and everything but the feel of her body against his.

Maeve gave herself to that kiss as she had never given herself before. Her head spun, and her feet seemed not to be connected to the world anymore. Then he released her, and she wanted only to be back in his embrace again.

"Will you, Maeve? Will you marry me and teach me not just to be part of a family again, but to love again? I want nothing more than to spend my life learning from you."

She wanted to cry, and to laugh, and to kiss him again. So she did the latter, and then she laughed.

"Am I such an amusing fellow? You have not answered," he said, a frown between his brows.

She smoothed that furrow with the lightest of touches, then said, "I was just thinking it would be so much nicer to have our midnight meetings in a more comfortable setting . . . such as in a bed, my lord."

"A marriage bed?" he asked.

She nodded, and now the tears began to slide down her cheeks, and he kissed each one's path.

Clarissa began to worry. It had grown so quiet in there. She bit her lip and shifted from one foot to the other, and then she crept to the window. Her mouth fell open at the sight of her uncle with his arms around Miss Midden, and him doing things she had only read of in books. She gaped openly, then pulled back, her cheeks flaming. It was a most compromising situation.

She grinned suddenly. It was going to be so much more fun to have an aunt—not a governess or a companion—take her into society next year.

Inside the inn, Maeve pulled back to smile into her lord's dark eyes. Her heart hammered in her chest. She did not think more joy existed in this world. "I suppose I will have to marry you."

"Yes, you will," he said, hunger in his voice and a glint in his eyes. "I am a gentleman and a lord of the realm, after all, and I could not do this to a woman unless I meant to marry her." And he went on to demonstrate in detail all the things a gentleman could not do to a lady without intending a long and lusty marriage.

AUTHOR'S NOTE

Setting *A Compromising Situation* in Yorkshire, in the rugged beauty of the Dales near the Gordale Scar, seemed a logical place, for I spent a very happy year of my life here. Indeed, Yorkshire rather runs in my blood. My father's mother came from Sheffield in South Yorkshire, and I felt quite at home on the moors or the green Dales. Much of my description came from memory, but I had help from Maurice Colbeck's book, *Yorkshire*, put out by B. T. Batsford Ltd., a UK publisher.

Readers may be interested to note that the Black Bear used in *A Compromising Situation* actually existed, and comes with its own unique bit of history. In the mid 1770s, the landlord of the Black Bear would proudly show off the sketches of his son to visitors when they stopped at the Devizes inn. By the time when *A Compromising Situation* is set, that boy had grown up to become the famous portrait painter of the fashionable Regency world—Sir Thomas Lawrence.

I love to hear from readers. Please write or e-mail me, and don't forget to ask for a free copy of a Regency recipe for Yorkshire Cakes (which are actually more like American biscuits): Shannon Donnelly, P.O. Box 3313, Burbank, CA 91508-3313; read@shannondonnelly.com; http:www.shannondonnelly.com.